365
Stories
and
Rhymes

igloobooks.com

Mary Had A Little Lamb

Mary had a little lamb,
Whose fleece was white as snow.
And everywhere that Mary went,
The lamb was sure to go.

He followed her to school one day,
That was against the rules.
It made the children laugh and play,
To see a lamb at school.

Have You Ever Seen A Lassie?

Have you ever seen a lassie, a lassie?
Have you seen a lassie go this way and that?
Go this way and that way, and this way and that way.
Have you ever seen a lassie go this way and that?

365
Stories
and
Rhymes

igloobooks.com

Mary Had A Little Lamb

Mary had a little lamb,
Whose fleece was white as snow.
And everywhere that Mary went,
The lamb was sure to go.

He followed her to school one day,
That was against the rules.
It made the children laugh and play,
To see a lamb at school.

Have You Ever Seen A Lassie?

Have you ever seen a lassie, a lassie?
Have you seen a lassie go this way and that?
Go this way and that way, and this way and that way.
Have you ever seen a lassie go this way and that?

Jack And Jill

Jack and Jill went up the hill,
To fetch a pail of water.
Jack fell down and broke his crown,
And Jill came tumbling after.

The Old Woman

There was an old woman who
lived under a hill,
And if she's not gone she lives there still.
Baked apples she sold, and cranberry pies,
And she's the old woman,
That never told lies.

Hey Diddle Diddle

Hey diddle diddle,
The cat and the fiddle,
The cow jumped over the moon.

The little dog laughed,
To see such fun,
And the dish ran away,
With the spoon!

Hark, Hark

Hark, Hark, the dogs go bark,
The beggars are coming to town.
Some in robes and some in rags,
And one in a velvet gown.

Pussycat Mole

Pussycat Mole,
Jumped over a coal,
And in her best petticoat,
Burnt a hole.

Pussycat Weeping

Poor pussy's weeping,
She'll have no more milk,
Until her best petticoat's
Mended with silk.

Two Cats Of Kilkenny

There once were two cats of Kilkenny,
Each thought there was one cat too many,
So they fought and they fit,
Til instead of two cats, there weren't any.

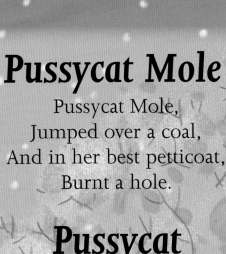

One For Sorrow

One for sorrow,
Two for joy,
Three for a girl,
Four for a boy,
Five for silver,
Six for gold,
Seven for a secret never to be told.
Eight for a wish,
Nine for a kiss,
Ten for a bird you should not miss.
Magpie!

Three Little Kittens

Three little kittens, they lost their mittens,
And they began to cry.
Oh, Mother, dear, we sadly fear,
Our mittens we have lost.
What! Lost your mittens? You naughty kittens!
Then you shall have no pie.
Mee-ow, mee-ow, mee-ow.

Ten Little Ladybirds

One little, two little, three little ladybirds,
Four little, five little, six little ladybirds,
Seven little, eight little, nine little ladybirds,
Ten little ladybird bugs.

One Little Ladybird

Ten little, nine little, eight little ladybirds,
Seven little, six little, five little ladybirds,
Four little, three little, two little ladybirds,
One little ladybird bug.

Six Little Mice

Six little mice sat down to spin,
Pussy passed by and she peeped in.
"What are you doing, my little men?"
"Weaving coats for gentlemen."
"Shall l come in and cut off your threads?"
"No, no, Mistress Pussy, you'd bite off our heads."
"Oh, no, I'll not; I'll help you to spin."
"That may be so,
But you don't
Come in!"

The Wheels On The Bus

The wheels on the bus go round and round,
Round and round, round and round.
The wheels on the bus go round and round,
All day long.

Little King Pippin

Little King Pippin, he built a great hall,
Pie-crust and pasty-crust, that was its wall.
The windows were made of black pudding and white,
And slated with pancakes, you never saw the like!

The Horn On The Bus

The horn on the bus goes toot toot toot,
Toot toot toot, toot toot toot.
The horn on the bus goes toot toot toot,
All day long.

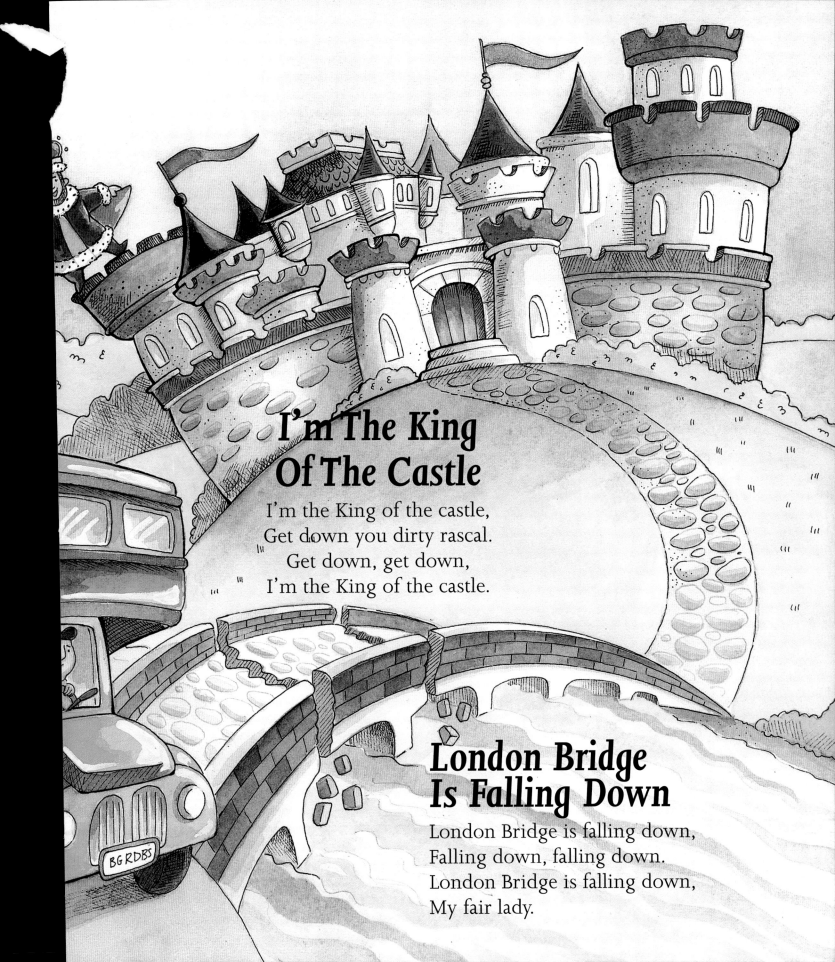

I'm The King Of The Castle

I'm the King of the castle,
Get down you dirty rascal.
Get down, get down,
I'm the King of the castle.

London Bridge Is Falling Down

London Bridge is falling down,
Falling down, falling down.
London Bridge is falling down,
My fair lady.

Old MacDonald

Old MacDonald had a farm, E-I-E-I-O.
And on that farm he had some ducks, E-I-E-I-O.
With a **quack quack** here and a **quack quack** there.
Here a **quack**, there a **quack**, everywhere a **quack, quack**.
Old MacDonald had a farm, E-I-E-I-O.

Six Little Ducks

Six little ducks that I once knew,
Fat ones, skinny ones, fair ones too.
But the one little duck with a feather on his back.
He led the others with his quack, quack, quack.
Quack, quack, quack,
Quack, quack, quack,
He led the others with his quack, quack, quack.

Duck's Ditty

All along the backwater,
Through the rushes tall,
Ducks are a-dabbling.
Up tails all!

Ducks' tails, drakes' tails,
Yellow feet a-quiver,
Yellow bills all out of sight,
Busy in the river!

Baa, Baa, Black Sheep

Baa, baa, black sheep,
Have you any wool?
Yes, sir, yes, sir,
Three bags full.
One for my master,
One for my dame,
And one for the little boy,
Who lives down the lane.

She Sells Sea Shells

She sells sea shells on the sea shore.
The shells she sells are sea shells, I'm sure.
And if she sells sea shells on the sea shore,
Then I'm sure she sells seashore shells.

Swan Swam

Swan swam over the sea,
Swim, swan, swim!
Swan swam back again,
Well swum, swan!

Ip Dip

Ip, dip,
Sky blue.
Who's it?
Not you!

A Sailor Went To Sea

A sailor went to sea, sea, sea,
To see what he could see, see, see,
And all that he could see, see, see,
Was the bottom of the deep blue sea, sea, sea.

If All The Seas Were One Sea

If all the seas were one sea, what a great sea that would be.

And if all the trees were one tree, what a great tree that would be.

And if all the axes were one axe, what a great axe that would be.

And if all the men were one man, what a great man that would be.

And if the great man took the great axe, and cut down the great tree.

And let it fall into the great sea, what a splish splash that would be.

Little Jack Horner

Little Jack Horner sat in the corner,
Eating a Christmas pie.
He put in his thumb,
And pulled out a plum,
And said, "What a good boy am I!"

Polly Put The Kettle On

Polly put the kettle on,
Polly put the kettle on,
Polly put the kettle on,
We'll all have tea.

Sukey take it off again,
Sukey take it off again,
Sukey take it off again,
They've all gone away.

Old Mother Hubbard

Old Mother Hubbard,
Went to the cupboard,
To give her poor dog a bone.
But when she got there,
The cupboard was bare,
And so the poor dog had none.

Come Let's To Bed

"Come, let's to bed," says Sleepy-head,
"Sit up a while," says Slow,
"Bang on the pot," says Greedy-Gut,
"We'll sup before we go."

I'm A Little Teapot

I'm a little teapot, short and stout,
Here is my handle, here is my spout,
When I get all steamed up, hear me shout,
Tip me over and pour me out.

Five Fat Sausages

Five fat sausages sizzling in a pan,
One went pop! And the others went bang!

Four fat sausages sizzling in a pan,
One went pop! And the others went bang!

Three fat sausages sizzling in a pan,
One went pop! And the others went bang!

Two fat sausages sizzling in a pan,
One went pop! And the other went bang!

One fat sausage sizzling in a pan
One went pop! And none went bang!

No fat sausages sizzling in a pan.

Sausage In A Pan

Sausage in a pan,
Sausage in a pan,
Turn 'em over, turn 'em over,
Sausage in a pan.

Little Tommy Tucker

Little Tommy Tucker,
Sings for his supper.
What shall we give him?
White bread and butter.
How shall he cut it without any knife?
How will he marry without any wife?

Peas And Honey

I eat my peas with honey,
I've done it all my life.
They do taste kind of funny,
But it keeps them on the knife.

Jack Sprat

Jack Sprat could eat no fat,
His wife could eat no lean,
And so between them both, you see,
They licked the platter clean.

Brush Your Teeth

Brush your teeth, brush your teeth,
Give them all a treat.
Brush up and down and all around,
To keep them clean and neat.

Bath Time

A rubber duck and a sailboat,
I watch my bath toys sink and float.
They keep me company in the tub,
Til Mother makes me soap and scrub.
I love to take a bath each night,
And go to bed all clean and bright.

Goosey, Goosey, Gander

Goosey, goosey, gander,
Wither shall I wander,
Upstairs and downstairs,
And in my lady's chamber.
There I met an old man,
Who would not say his prayers.
I took him by the left leg,
And threw him down the stairs.

As I Was Walking Up The Stair

As I was walking up the stair,
I met a man that wasn't there.
He wasn't there again today,
I wish, I wish he'd go away.

Ding Dong Bell

Ding dong bell.
Pussy's in the well.
Who put her in?
Little Tommy Thin.
Who pulled her out?
Little Tommy Stout.
What a naughty boy was that,
To drown poor pussy cat,
Who never did any harm,
But killed all the mice in father's barn.

Farewell

Farewell to old England forever,
Farewell to my old pals as well,
Farewell to the well-known Old Baile
Where I used to look such a swell.

One Man Went To Mow

One man went to mow,
Went to mow a meadow,
One man and his dog,
Went to mow a meadow.

Oats, Peas, Beans And Barley

Oats, peas, beans and barley grow,
Oats, peas, beans and barley grow,
Can you, or I, or anyone know,
How oats, peas, beans and barley grow?
First the farmer sows the seed,
Then he stands and takes his ease,
He stamps his foot and claps his hands,
And turns around to view his land.

Little Boy Blue

Little Boy Blue, come, blow your horn!
The sheep's in the meadow, the cow's in the corn.
Where's the little boy that looks after the sheep?
Under the haystack, fast asleep.

Little Polly Flinders

Little Polly Flinders,
Sat among the cinders,
Warming her pretty little toes.

Her mother came and caught her,
And told her little daughter off,
For spoiling her nice new clothes.

Doodle, Doodle, Doo

Doodle, doodle, doo,
The princess lost her shoe.
Her highness hopped,
The fiddler stopped,
Not knowing what to do.

Jumping Joan

Here I am,
Little Jumping Joan.
When nobody's with me,
I'm all alone!

The Farmer Wants A Wife

The farmer wants a wife,
The farmer wants a wife,
E-I-E-I-O, the farmer wants a wife.

The wife wants a child,
The wife wants a child,
E-I-E-I-O, the wife wants a child.

The child wants a nurse,
The child wants a nurse,
E-I-E-I-O, the child wants a nurse.

The Farmer In The Dell

The farmer in the dell,
The farmer in the dell,
Hi-ho, the derry-o,
The farmer in the dell.

The farmer has a dog,
The farmer has a dog,
Hi-ho, the derry-o,
The farmer has a dog.

The Cock Crows

The cock crows in the morn,
To tell us to rise,
And he that lies late,
Will never be wise.

Over The Hills

Tom, he was a piper's son,
He learned to play,
when he was young.
And all the tune,
that he could play,
Was, "Over the hills,
A great way off,
The wind shall blow,
My top knot off."

Little Bo-Peep

Little Bo-Peep has lost her sheep,
And can't tell where to find them.
Leave them alone, and they'll come home,
And bring their tails behind them.

The Ants Go Marching

The ants go marching one by one,
Hurray! Hurray!
The ants go marching one by one,
Hurray! Hurray!
The ants go marching one by one,
The little one stops to suck her thumb,
And they all go marching down,
To the ground,
To get out, of the rain,
Boom, boom, boom, boom!

High In The Pine Tree

High in the pine tree,
The little turtledove,
Made a little nursery,
To please her little love.
"Coo," said the turtledove,
"Coo," said she,
In the long shady branches,
Of the dark pine tree.

Rain On The Green Grass

Rain on the green grass,
And rain on the tree.
Rain on the roof-top,
But not on me.

Jenny Wren

As little Jenny Wren,
Was sitting by the shed.
She waggled with her tail,
And nodded with her head.

She waggled with her tail,
And nodded with her head.
As little Jenny Wren,
Was sitting by the shed.

Whether The Weather

Whether the
weather be fine,
Or whether the weather be not,
Wether the
weather be cold,
Or wether the
weather be hot,
We'll weather
the weather,
Whatever the weather,
Whether we like it not!

An Apple A Day

An apple a day,
Sends the doctor away.

An apple in the morning,
Doctor's warning!

Roast apple at night,
Starves the doctor outright.

Doctor Foster

Doctor Foster went to Gloucester,
In a shower of rain.
He stepped in a puddle,
Right up to his middle,
And never went there again.

Doctor Bell

Doctor Bell,
Fell down the well,
And broke his
collar bone.
Doctors should
Attend the sick,
And leave the
well alone.

John Jacob Jingleheimer

John Jacob Jingleheimer Schmidt,
His name is my name, too.
Whenever we go out,
The people always shout,
There goes John Jacob Jingleheimer Schmidt.

Cackle, Cackle

Cackle, cackle, Mother Goose,
Have you any feathers loose?
Truly have I, pretty fellow,
Half enough to fill a pillow.
Here are quills, take one or two,
And down to make a bed for you.

The Clever Hen

I had a little hen, the prettiest ever seen,
She washed the dishes and kept the house clean.
She went to the mill to fetch me some flour,
She brought it home in less than an hour.
She baked me my bread, she brewed me my ale,
She sat by the fire and told many a fine tale.

A Cat Came Fiddling

A cat came fiddling out of a barn,
With a pair of bagpipes under her arm.
She could sing nothing but fiddle dee dee,
The mouse has married the bumblebee.
Pipe cat, dance mouse,
We'll have a wedding at our good house.

Higgelty, Piggelty, Pop!

Higgelty, piggelty, pop!
The dog has eaten the mop.
The pig's in a hurry,
The cat's in a flurry,
Higgelty, piggelty, pop!

The Bell on the Bus

Suzy, Jonny, Derek and Dot were all waiting for the bus. "Here it comes," said Dot excitedly. "Put out your hand, everyone! That's how the bus driver knows that we want him to stop." The bus driver saw them waiting with their hands out. He slowed the bright, red bus down and stopped next to the green sign. The friends all cheered and climbed aboard.

Derek, Jonny, Dot and Suzy all held on tightly as the bus swung around corners, to the left and to the right. Next, the bus stopped to pick up Pete and his mommy, Milly. "We're off into town," said Milly to the bus driver. She paid both hers and Pete's fares, while Pete ran to find them a seat.

The bright, red bus was getting very full. As it reached the blue bus stop, Walter was waiting there with his arm out. "Oh my," he said as he climbed aboard. "It's very busy on the bus today." There wasn't a even seat free for Walter. Derek very kindly stood up and offered Walter his seat.

It was a bit of a squash on board the bus, but soon, they reached the town. "Hurray," cheered all the passengers. "We're here at last!" Everyone got off the bus and said goodbye to the bus driver.

The bus driver smiled and rang his bell. He'd be back to pick them up very soon!

Dressing-Up Magic

Katie was really excited when her mother brought home a fairy wand for her. She loved dressing up. "Thank you!" cried Katie as she waved the wand around. "Do you think it's magic?"

"There's one way to find out," replied her mother. "Why don't you make a wish?" So, Katie waved her magic wand.

"I wish that Jenny would come and play today," she cried.
Suddenly, the doorbell rang. It was Jenny. "Can you play?" she asked.

Katie was amazed. "Yes!" she replied. "Come in and see what I've got!"
She twirled her wand. "Mom bought it for me," she said.
"Oh, how lovely!" cried Jenny. "It's magic," whispered Katie, smiling.

The two friends hurried up to Katie's bedroom. "Do you have any dressing-up clothes?" asked Jenny. "I'd love to be a fairy princess."

"No," replied Katie. Then, she smiled. "I wish we could be fairy princesses!" she said, waving her wand. Suddenly, her mother opened the door. "Look what I found!" she said, holding out two floaty dresses with fairy wings attached.

Jenny and Katie danced around the bedroom. They twirled around and danced out into the hallway. Wearing their dresses and waving their wands, they felt like the prettiest fairy princesses in the world.

Katie's kitten, Patch, joined in the fun, too. "I love being a fairy," Jenny said, as Patch ran around her feet. Katie agreed. "It's the most magical fun," she giggled, with a wave of her wonderful wand.

Amy's Game

Amy loved to play games with her dad before bedtime. One night, Amy said to her dad, "Let's play hide-and-seek."

"Ok," he said with a chuckle. "I'll count from one to ten, and you find somewhere to hide. I'll cover my eyes and I promise I won't peek. Ready, steady, go!"

Once Amy's dad had counted to ten, he opened his eyes. Amy was nowhere to be seen. He checked under the bed and in the wardrobe and behind the door. She wasn't hiding in any of those places, though. "Where are you, Amy?" he asked. "I'm coming to find you!"

Dad lifted up the lid of Amy's little green toy box. She wasn't hiding there. Then, he opened all the drawers in her room. He looked through the sock drawer and the t-shirt drawer and the pajama draw. But he still couldn't find Amy.

Just then, Amy's dad heard a giggling coming from Amy's bed. He saw a tail poking out from under the quilt. So he crept across the carpet and shouted, 'BOO!' right next to Amy's pillow.

Amy jumped up with a squeal as her dad said, "I found you!" Amy giggled and giggled. Hide-and-seek was definitely her favorite game of all.

What Are You Doing, Dennis?

Dennis and his family had gone to the park for a lovely picnic. "Come on, Lola," said Dennis to his sister. "We're going to go exploring." He got out his big magnifying glass. "Ah, ha!" said Dennis. "Look what I've found."

"Let me see," said Lola and she crouched down to have a look. "Ugh, it's a big fat snake!"

Dennis tried to tell her it was only a worm, but she had already run away. "What are you doing, Dennis?" called their mother. "Nothing!" he replied.

In a leafy hedge, a spider had spun his web and was sitting right in the middle of it. So, Dennis showed it to Lola with his big magnifying glass.

Lola stared, at the long, hairy legs and the big, hairy body. "It's a monster," she cried. Then, suddenly, the big web wobbled and the huge spider moved. "The monster's going to eat us!" shrieked Lola. "I want Mother."
Just then, Mum called out, "The picnic's ready."

"Help me!" cried Lola, running over. to the picnic "I've seen a scary snake and a monster that moved. He was as big as a house and he nearly got me!"

"Don't worry, Lola," soothed their mother, "There aren't really any monsters. It's just Dennis playing a game with you."

"What have you been saying to your little sister?" asked Dad.
"Nothing," said Dennis, slipping his magnifying glass back into his rucksack.

He sat down and looked at all the delicious food on the picnic rug.
Then, Dennis gave a cheeky smile and took a big bite of his favorite sandwich.

Danny And The Dinosaur

Danny had a pet dinosaur called Rex. He was very big and very friendly. Rex followed Danny everywhere, but he wasn't allowed to sleep in Danny's bedroom at night.

There was one problem, though. Even though Rex was a big dinosaur, he was afraid of sleeping outside in the dark. Every night, Rex would want to stay in Danny's room. "You're not allowed, Rex," Danny would say, when Rex looked at him with big, sad eyes.

One night, Rex slept very badly. He had terrible nightmares about being trapped inside a big, fluffy cloud. In the morning, when he woke up, Danny saw that Rex had chewed his pillow to bits in his sleep.

"Oh, Rex, you silly dinosaur," said Danny, as the neighbours pointed and laughed. Danny felt very sorry for Rex, so he started to hatch a plan.

The next day, Danny asked his mother and father if Rex could sleep inside. Danny told them all about Rex's nightmares and, eventually, they agreed.

"Rex!" called Danny from his window that evening. "How would you like to sleep inside tonight?" Rex thought it was the best idea he had ever heard.

That night, Rex slept better than ever before, safely snuggled up in Danny's bedroom. The neighbours couldn't laugh at him anymore and he didn't have a single nightmare.

Danny was happy that Rex could sleep soundly at last. As Rex drifted off, Danny started to fall asleep too. There was one thing that Danny hadn't counted on, though. A dinosaur is very loud when he snores!

Carrie The Climber

Carrie's brother, Ben, had climbed up to the tree house in their garden. "I want to climb up, too," said Carrie. But, Ben pulled up the ladder and said, "No, Carrie, you can't come up."

"You're too small to climb the ladder," said Dad. "It's a little bit too high," said Carrie's mother.

But, Carrie was determined to climb up to the tree house.

She started to think of different ways that she could make it up to the tree house. There must be something that she could climb on to reach the lowest tree branch. Suddenly, she had a great idea.

So, when no one was looking, Carrie went to the shed and pulled out her play chair and her plastic toy box. "I'll be big enough to climb up, now," she said.

Carrie climbed onto the box and then onto the chair.
"I'm nearly there," she said and she gave a little kick. But, the chair slipped and fell with a *thunk,* onto the grass. "Help!" cried Carrie. "I'm stuck!"

Ben looked down and Mother looked up. Then, Dad ran as fast as he could to the bottom of the tree. He reached up to Carrie and said, "Hold on to me." Soon, Carrie was safe and sound, back on the ground.

"It is important to listen to what we say," said Mother.
"Sorry, Mother," said Carrie. "But, one day, I'm going to be a very good tree climber." Everyone smiled. "We know you will," they said.

Walter To The Rescue

Walter the Giraffe was playing at the park with his friends, but he wasn't very happy. "What's the matter, Walter?" asked his best friend, Josh.

"You're all having loads of playing on everything," sighed Walter. "But, I'm too big for the climbing frame, I'm not having any fun at all."

"Why don't you have a go on the slide?" asked Sammy. But, when Walter got onto the slide, his long legs nearly reached the bottom. He couldn't go whooshing down the slide like all the others. "You see?" said Walter, feeling very annoyed, "I'm just too big to have fun."

Suddenly, there was a loud cry. "Help, help," said a voice. "I'm stuck!"

It was Walter's friend, Elly. She had climbed right up to the top of the climbing frame, but now she was too frightened to climb back down.

Walter quickly went over on his long, graceful legs. He could easily reach the top of the climbing frame. "Don't worry, Elly," he said. "Climb on to my neck and I'll lower you down."

So, Elly climbed onto Walter's neck and she was soon safely on the ground. Everyone cheered and said, "Hooray for Walter!"

"Thank you for rescuing me, Walter," said Elly. "It's a good job you've got long legs and a long neck." Walter felt shy. He even went a little bit red. "Maybe it's not so bad being me after all," he said, with a big smile.

The King Who Couldn't Sleep

There once was a very kind king, who would help his servants with their chores. He always had trouble sleeping and he found that doing the chores helped him to sleep better.

One night, he went to see the royal treasure keeper in his pajamas. "I can't get to sleep," complained the king. "Let me help you polish some of the treasure."

The king helped the royal treasure keeper with his polishing, until he had all the diamonds dazzling, the sapphires sparkling and the gold coins glittering like the sun.

"Thank you for finishing my work," yawned the treasure keeper, pulling on his nightcap. "I'm off to bed, your majesty. Goodnight." The king still wasn't tired though, so he went to the royal kitchen.

In the castle kitchen, the cook was busy kneading dough to make delicious, fresh bread for breakfast. "I can't sleep," moaned the king.

"You've come to the right place," said the cook. "I always need a nap after kneading the bread dough. It's very tiring." The king was soon surrounded by a fog of flour, as he pushed and pressed the dough. Although he worked very hard, he still felt wide awake.

Finally, the king went back upstairs to see the queen. "I can't get to sleep,"
he sniffed, feeling very sorry for himself, "No one can help me."

"Don't be silly," said the queen. She fetched him a cup of hot milk.

The king took a sip and said, "I think I'll just snuggle down for a minute."
The queen was just about to read him a bedtime story when she heard a soft,
snoring sound. After helping with such difficult chores, the wide-awake king
was finally fast asleep.

Meg's Adventure

Meg lived with her mother near a big wood. "Can I play in the wood today?" asked Meg. Meg's mother shook her head and said, "You can't go into the woods by yourself, Meg. I'm too busy to go with you today."

Meg felt a bit disappointed, so she went next door to see if her best friend, Mimi, wanted to play.

Meg and Mimi played catch and had great fun. But then, the ball rolled right up to the edge of the wood. "It looks so lovely and pretty in there," said Meg. "I'm not by myself, so I'm sure Mother wouldn't mind if we played in the woods for a little bit." So, she stepped into the trees with Mimi following behind.

Soon, they had wandered far into the wood. Meg looked around and asked, "Where are we?"
"I don't know," replied Mimi, "but I want to go home now, I'm scared."

Meg was a bit scared, too. But then, she heard someone calling.
"Meg, Mimi, where are you?" It was Meg's mother. She had come to look for Meg and Mimi.

"I told you not to go off into the wood," said Meg's mother, hugging them both tight. Meg told her that they hadn't meant to wander so far into the wood. Meg's mother hugged them and said, "Never mind, Meg. The important thing is that you're safe now."

Meg and Mimi both smiled. Then, Meg's mother held their hands. "Come on, you two," she said. "Let's go home and we'll all play together."

Jack and The Beanstalk

Once upon a time, a poor window lived with her only son, Jack. Jack and his mother never had any money and their only possession was a black and white cow. "We shall have to sell the cow," said Jack's mother one day, sadly. "Take her to market and get the best price you can for her."

One the way to market, Jack met a strange looking man. "That's a fine cow you have there," said the man. "Will you sell her to me for these magic beans?"

The magic beans sounded very exciting. So, Jack exchanged the cow for the beans and went home.

When Jack's mother heard what he had done, she was furious. She threw the beans out of the window and sent Jack to bed.

The next morning, Jack woke up and looked out of his window. In the tiny garden, an enormous beanstalk had sprouted from the beans. It led right up into the clouds. Jack was curious to know what was at the top, so he began to climb it.

When Jack reached the top, he found a huge castle, built on top of the clouds. He snuck through the castle door. But just as he started to explore the castle, he heard great, thumping footsteps. It was the giant who lived in the castle.

Jack sneaked inside a huge oven and watched. The giant was carrying three big bags of gold. Suddenly, he sniffed the air and bellowed,

"Fee, fi, fo, fum,
I smell the blood of an Englishman.
Be he alive, or be he dead,
I'll grind his bones to make my bread!"

The giant searched everywhere for Jack, but he didn't look in the oven. Eventually, the giant sat at his kitchen table and fell asleep. Jack opened the oven door and crept out. He grabbed one of the bags of money and sneaked back to the beanstalk, then climbed down carefully. His mother was delighted to see him and they had enough money to live on for many months.

However, eventually, the money ran out. "I must climb the beanstalk to the castle again," said Jack and he climbed to the top of the beanstalk once more. The giant was out again but, on his enormous kitchen table was a beautiful hen. Jack was about to snatch it, when he heard the giant return. The giant cried,

"Fee, fi, fo, fum,
I smell the blood of an Englishman.
Be he alive, or be he dead,
I'll grind his bones to make my bread!"

Jack hid in a giant mousehole, so the giant could not find him. The giant sat at the table and pulled out a little golden harp and started to play it. Suddenly, the hen laid an egg of pure gold. The giant leaned back on his chair in satisfaction and was soon fast asleep.

Jack came out of his hiding place, put the hen under his arm and crept out of the kitchen. Suddenly, the hen let out a loud squawk. The giant woke up with a start and saw that his hen was gone, but Jack was already charging back to the beanstalk.

At home, Jack tried to get the hen to lay a golden egg, but it just clucked, sadly. "We need the golden harp," said Jack. So he climbed the beanstalk one more time, until he was back in the land above the clouds. Searching through the giant's house, Jack found the harp in an enormous cupboard. Just as he was about to creep away with it, he heard the giant bellowing,

"Fee, fi, fo, fum,
I smell the blood of an Englishman.
Be he alive, or be he dead,
I'll grind his bones to make my bread!"

Jack grabbed the harp and ran out of the castle with it. However, the harp was magical and could speak. "I'm being stolen!" it cried out.

The giant thundered after Jack who ran as fast as he could, for fear that he would be caught and his bones ground up to make the giant's bread.

At last, Jack reached the beanstalk and climbed down. Behind him, the giant jumped onto the beanstalk and began climbing down, too.

So, once Jack reached the ground he fetched an axe. He chopped and chopped at the bottom of the beanstalk with all his might, until it wobbled and crashed down. The giant fell to the ground and was so shocked, he ran away and never came back. With the back of money, Jack and his mother were never poor again and they lived happily ever after.

Picture Perfect

Suzy loved painting. She painted pictures of everything, but she especially liked to paint her dog, Scruffy. He was a lovely dog, but he was very messy

Suzy had almost finished her entry for the village painting competition, when Scruffy stepped in red and blue paint and walked all over her picture. It was covered in doggy footprints.

"What am I going to do?" wailed Suzy. "My painting's ruined. I can't enter the competition now."

"Just take that one to the show," said her mother. "It's still lovely."

Suzy didn't think it was lovely at all, but she really wanted to enter the competition. Since the show started in five minutes, she had no choice.

When Suzy got to the show, she was suddenly very worried that her painting wouldn't fit in with all the others. "I hope they don't laugh at my picture," she said to her mother, as they walked in.

"Of course they won't," Suzy's mother replied with a smile. Suzy smiled and felt a little better, but she was still very nervous as she handed her picture to the judges.

Soon, it was the time for the results to be announced. Suzy clapped, as the winner and the person in second place both got prizes.

"Third place goes to... Suzy and her painting of Scruffy!" said the judge, handing Suzy a prize. It was a brand new sketch pad.

Suzy couldn't believe that Scruffy had helped her win a prize. "Well done, Scruffy," she said, as everyone clapped and cheered. Scruffy wagged his tail happily. He was good at painting after all!

Fiona's Post

Fiona didn't like it when the postman came to deliver letters and parcels to her house. She would hear the garden gate creak open and slam shut.
Then he would crunch along the garden path, carrying a big bag full of mail.

When she saw the postman through the window, Fiona thought that he looked really scary. He was huge and he had a dark grey shadow. Usually, when the postman came to the door, Fiona would run upstairs to her bedroom and hide.

One morning, the postman rang the bell and Fiona ran to hide under the stairs. "Hello," he said, when Fiona's mother opened the door. "I've got a very special parcel for you today." Fiona's mother took the box out of his hands and called Fiona over.

"Open the box," Fiona's mother told her. "It's got your name on it!"
Fiona did as she was told and inside the box she found a birthday present.

"It's a present," her mother said. "Because today is your birthday, remember?"
Fiona giggled. She had been so scared of the postman that she had completely
forgotten. From then on, she was never afraid of the postman again..

Brave Bonny

One day, Bonny was helping her dad to prepare a party for Olly's birthday. Suddenly, outside, thunder crashed and lightning flashed. "I don't like it," said Bonny, and she covered her ears and began to cry.

"Bonny's a cry-baby and she's not brave," teased her little brother, Olly. "That's not true, Olly," said Dad, "Just because Bonny is afraid, it doesn't mean she isn't brave."

That afternoon, everyone came round for the party. There were sandwiches and jelly and lots of party games. Bonny forgot all about the thunderstorm. She was having a lovely time when suddenly, there was a very loud, BANG!

With one great leap, Bonny dived under the table, making the jelly wobble and the plates clatter. "Silly, Bonny," giggled Olly, "It's just a balloon bursting." Poor Bonny felt very silly.

The next day, Bonny and Olly were at the park, playing in the sandpit. Suddenly, two older boys crowded around Olly and started to make fun of him.

Bonny was very angry that they were picking on her little brother. She ran at them as fast as she could. "What are you doing?" she shouted. "Leave my little brother alone!" The bullies quickly ran away because Bonny looked so angry.

"They wouldn't let me play in the sandpit," said Olly. "They said it was theirs." Bonny smiled kindly at her brother and gave him a hug.

"Well it isn't," she replied. "It is for everyone to play in." Then, she took Olly by the hand and led him back to Dad.

Dad was very proud of Bonny for sticking up for her little brother. "Well," said Dad, "I think Bonny was very brave, don't you, Olly?" he asked. "Yes," said Olly, giving Bonny a big hug. "I'm sorry I laughed at you when you were afraid," he said. "I think you're the bravest sister ever."

Captain Percy

Captain Black Bear was the captain of the pirate ship, The Black Claw.
He was fierce and mean. He hoarded any treasure that the pirates stole and
made them work very hard on the ship. They had to scrub the deck, make his
food and hoist the heavy mainsail. Captain Black Bear, however, never did any
work himself.

The captain's parrot, Percy, was just as unhappy as the crew. All day long, he
sat on his master's shoulder. If he squawked, he was told to be quiet.
Percy was tired of being bossed around all day long.

"Captain Black Bear never does anything," thought Percy. "If only we could
have another captain. We need someone clever and adventurous, but who also
treats the crew kindly. Someone like me!"

Percy thought and thought until he came up with a plan. He waited until Black Bear wasn't looking, then stole the key to the treasure room.

Later on, when the captain was inspecting his treasure, Percy grabbed Black Bear's hat and his long cutlass. He squawked as loudly as he could and flapped out of the door.

"What are you doing, you feathered fool!" roared Black Bear. Percy just squawked and slammed the door, then locked it behind him. The fearsome captain was trapped.

Percy quickly flew up on deck and called to the crew. "At last we are free of Captain Black Bear!" he squawked.

The crew cheered. "What did you do with him, Percy?" asked Tim the Turtle. Percy told him that he had locked Black Bear in the treasure room. "Hurray," everyone shouted. "When we reach land, we'll leave him there!"

Percy squawked again. "I'd like to be your captain," he said to the crew. "If you let me, I promise to do my fair share of the work and to share out all the treasure we find."

Everyone agreed that Percy would make a wonderful captain. The crew and their new captain celebrated with a big party. They ate lovely food and drank coconut milk. From then on, The Black Claw was the jolliest of all pirate ships on the Seven Seas. Captain Percy kept his word and shared all the treasure equally between the crew. No one ever heard of mean old Black Bear again.

Bathtime for Bo

One lovely, sunny morning, Baby Bo was curled up in her bed. Her mom came into her room and woke her up.

"Good morning, sleepy-head!" she said to Bo. "It's time for you to have a bath!" Bo's mom took her into the bathroom. Then, she got a big bath towel and turned on the taps.

The bath water swooshed and splashed into the tub. It swirled all around and lots of bubbles began to appear. Bo put her little rubber duck under the water and he bobbed to the surface. He looked just like a real duck swimming along in a pond, Bo thought happily.

Next, Bo's mom put her in the tub, into the lovely warm bath water. She got the dolphin-shaped soap and washed Bo all over with it. Bo giggled because the soap tickled and because her mom was pulling lots of funny faces. In no time at all, Bo was nice and clean!

"All done," said Bo's mom, as she lifted Bo out of the bath. With the big, fluffy bath towel, she dried Bo from top to toe. She dressed Bo in a pink and green babygro and wiped the bubbles off her nose.

Then Bo's mom patted the rubber duck dry with the towel. "Look, Bo," she said. "He's had a bath, just like you!"

Solomon Grundy

Solomon Grundy,
Born on a Monday,
Christened on Tuesday,
Married on Wednesday,
Took ill on Thursday,
Worse on Friday,
Died on Saturday,
Buried on Sunday,
This is the end,
Of Solomon Grundy.

Tommy Snooks

As Tommy Snooks and Bessy Brooks,
Were walking out one Sunday.
Says Tommy Snooks to Bessy Brooks,
"Will you marry me on Monday?"

Bessy Bell And Mary Gray

Bessy Bell and Mary Gray,
They were two bonny lasses.
They built their house upon the lea,
And covered it with rashes.

Bessy kept the garden gate,
And Mary kept the pantry.
Bessy always had to wait,
While Mary lived in plenty.

IF I Were A Cabbage

If I were a cabbage,
I'd split myself in two.
I'd give my leaves to others,
But give my heart to you.

IF I Were A Sole

If I were a sole,
And you a peice of leather,
I'd ask an old cobbler,
To sew us together.

Pop! Goes The Weasel

All around the carpenter's bench,
The monkey chased the weasel.
That's the way,
The monkey goes,
Pop! Goes the weasel.

How Much Wood

How much wood would a woodchuck chuck,
If a woodchuck could chuck wood?
He would chuck, he would, as much as he could,
And chuck as much wood as a woodchuck would,
If a woodchuck could chuck wood.

Cross Patch

Cross Patch,
Draw the latch,
Sit by the fire and spin.
Take a cup and drink it up,
Then call your neighbors in.

I Love Sixpence

I love sixpence, pretty little sixpence,
I love sixpence better than my life.
I spent a penny of it, I spent another,
And I took fourpence,
Home to my wife.

The House That Jack Built

This is the house,
That Jack built.

This is the malt,
That lay in the house,
That Jack built.

This is the rat,
That ate the malt,
That lay in the house,
That Jack built.

This is the cat,
That killed the rat,
That ate the malt,
That lay in the house,
That Jack built.

Where, Oh Where

Where, oh where,
Has my little dog gone?
Where, oh where, can he be?
With his tail cut short,
And his ears cut long,
Where, oh where,
Has he gone?

B-I-N-G-O

There was a farmer who had a dog,
And Bingo was his name-o,
B-I-N-G-O,
B-I-N-G-O,
B-I-N-G-O,
And Bingo was his name-o.

There's A Hole In My Bucket

There's a hole in my bucket,
Dear Liza, dear Liza,
There's a hole in my bucket,
Dear Liza, a hole.

The fix it, dear Henry,
Dear Henry, dear Henry,
Then fix it dear Henry,
Dear Henry, fix it.

Five Green And Speckled Frogs

Five green and speckled frogs,
Sat on a speckled log,
Eating some most delicious bugs.
One jumped into the pool,
Where it was nice and cool,
Then there were four
Green speckled frogs.

Down At The Station

Down at the station, early in the morning.
See the little puffer trains, all in a row.
Here comes the driver to start up the engine,
Puff puff! Peep peep! Off we go!

The Runaway Train

The runaway train went over the hill and she blew,
The runaway train went over the hill and she blew,
The runaway train went over the hill,
And the last we heard she was going still,
And she blew, blew, blew, blew, blew.

Wind The Bobbin Up

Wind the bobbin up,
Wind the bobbin up,
Pull, pull, clap, clap, clap.
Point to the window, point to the door,
Clap your hands together, one two three,
Put your hands upon your knee.

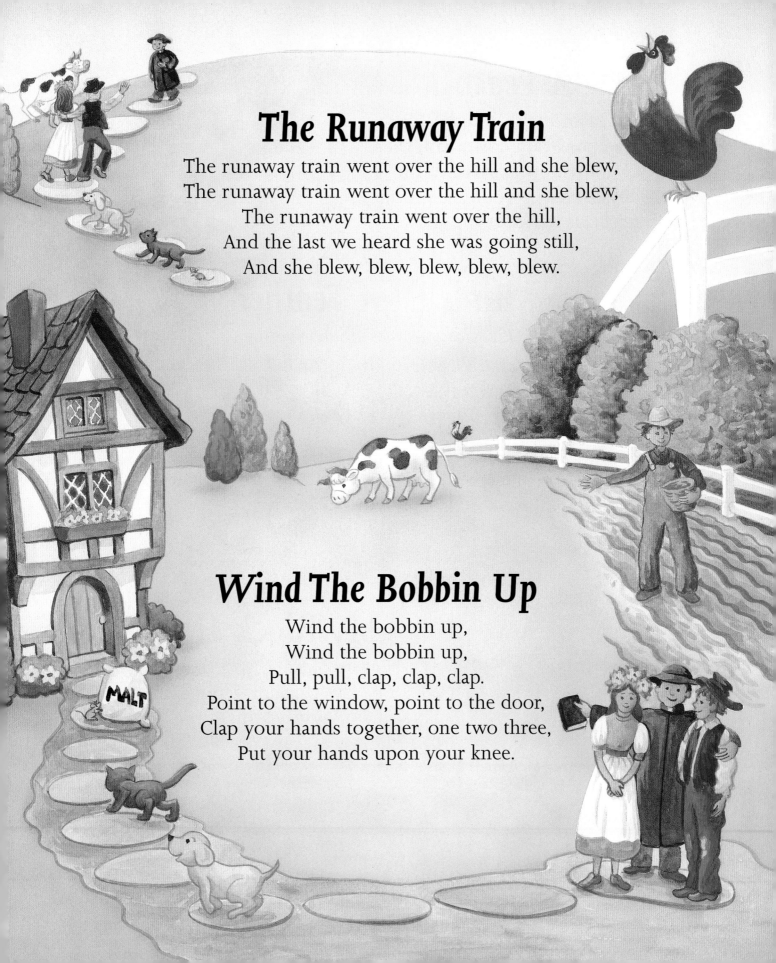

I Saw A Peacock

I saw a peacock with a fiery tail,
I saw a comet rain down hail,
I saw a cloud with ivy circled round,
And a mighty oak creep upon the ground.

Birds Of A Feather

Birds of a feather flock together,
And so do pigs and swine.
Rats and mice will have their choice,
And so will l have mine.

My Black Hen

Hickety pickety, my black hen,
She lays eggs for gentlemen,
Sometimes nine, sometimes ten,
Hickety pickety, my black hen.

Animal Fair

I went to the animal fair,
The birds and the beasts were there,
The big baboon by the light of the moon,
Was combing his auburn hair.

You ought to have seen the monkey,
He jumped on the elephant's trunk.
The elephant sneezed and fell on his knees,
And what became of the monkey?

When The Saints Go Marching In

Oh when the saints,
Go marching in,
Oh when the saints go marching in,
I want to be in that number,
When the saints go marching in!

I Had A Little Nut Tree

I had a little nut tree,
Nothing would it bear,
But a silver nutmeg,
And a golden pear.
The King of Spain's daughter,
Came to visit me.
And all for the sake,
Of my little nut tree.

The Grand Old Duke Of York

The grand old Duke of York,
 He had ten thousand men.
 He marched them up to the top of the hill,
And he marched them down again.

And when they were up, they were up,
And when they were down, they were down,
And when they were only halfway up,
They were neither up nor down!

Who Killed Cock Robin?

Who killed Cock Robin?
 "I," said the sparrow,
 "With my bow and arrow,
 I killed Cock Robin."

I Had A Little Pony

I had a little pony, his name was Dapple Gray.
I lent him to a lady to ride a mile away.
She whipped him, she thrashed him,
She rode him through the mire.
Now I would not lend my pony,
To any lady hire.

The Ladies Ride

This is the way the ladies ride,
Tri, tre, tre, tree!
Tri, tre, tre, tree!
This is the way the ladies ride,
Tri, tre, tre, tre, tri-tre-tre-tree!

The Gentlemen Ride

This is the way the gentlemen ride,
Gallop-a-trot!
Gallop-a-trot!
This is the way the gentlemen ride,
Gallop-a-gallop-a-trot!

A Farmer Went Trotting

A farmer went trotting upon his bay mare,
Bumpety, bumpety, bump!
With his daughter behind, so rosy and fair,
Bumpety, bumpety, bump!
A raven cried, "Croak!" and they went tumbling down,
Bumpety, bumpety, bump!

Curly Locks

Curly Locks, Curly Locks,
Will you be mine?
You shall not wash dishes,
Or feed the swine.
But sit on a cushion,
And feed upon strawberries,
Sugar and cream.

Star Light, Star Bright

Star light, star bright,
The first star I see tonight,
I wish I may, I wish I might,
Have the wish I wish tonight.

The Sandman

The Sandman's coming,
In his train of cars,
With moonbeam windows,
And with wheels of stars.
So hush you little ones,
And have no fear,
The man-in-the-moon,
He's the engineer.

Sleep, Baby, Sleep

Sleep, baby, sleep,
Your father tends the sheep,
Your mother shakes the dreamland tree,
And from it fall sweet dreams for thee.
Sleep, baby, sleep.
Sleep, baby, sleep.

The Man In The Moon

The man in the moon came tumbling down,
And asked the way to Norwich.
He went by the south, and burnt his mouth,
With eating cold pease porridge.

The Railroad Track

The railroad track 'tis a moonbeam bright,
That leads right up into the starry night.
So come you little ones,
And run up the stairs,
Put on your 'jamas and say your prayers.

Early To Bed

Early to bed,
Early to rise.
Makes little Johnny,
Wealthy and wise.

Simple Simon

Simple Simon met a pieman,
Going to the fair.
Says Simple Simon to the pieman,
"Let me taste your ware."

Says the pieman to Simple Simon,
"Show me first your penny,"
Says Simple Simon to the pieman,
"Indeed, I have not any."

ABC, Apple Pie

Says A, give me a good large slice,
Says B, a little bit, but nice,
Says C, cut me a piece of crust,
Take it, says D, it's dry as dust.

Scarborough Fair

Are you going to Scarborough Fair?
Parsley, sage, rosemary and thyme,
Remember me to one who lives there,
For once she was a true love of mine.

Up The Wooden Hill

Up the wooden hill to Blanket Fair,
What shall we have when we get there?
A bucket full of water,
And a penny-worth of hay,
Gee up, Dobbin, all the way!

Girls Are Dandy

Girls are dandy, made of candy,
That's what little girls are made of.
Boys are rotten, made of cotton,
That's what little boys are made of.

Incy Wincy Spider

Incy wincy spider climbed up the water spout,
Down came the rain and washed the spider out,
Out came the sun and dried up all the rain,
So incy wincy spider climbed up the spout again.

Green Grow The Rushes

I'll sing you one, oh.
Green grow the rushes, oh.
What is your one, oh?
One is one and all alone,
And evermore shall be it so.

I Saw A Mouse

I saw a mouse!
Where?
There on the stair!
Where on the stair?
Right there!
A little mouse with clogs on.
Well, I decare!
Going clippety-clop on the stair.

The Crooked Sixpence

There was a crooked man, and he went a crooked mile,
He found a crooked sixpence beside a crooked stile,
He bought a crooked cat, which caught a crooked mouse,
And they all lived together in a little crooked house.

Girl Guide

I'm a Girl Guide in pink and blue,
These are the actions I must do.
Salute to the Captain,
Bow to the Queen,
And turn my back,
To the boy in green.

My Head

This is the circle,
That is my head.
This is my mouth,
With which words are said.
These are my eyes,
With which I see.
This is my nose,
That's a part of me.
This is the hair,
That grows on my head.
And this is my hat,
All pretty and red.

Bat, Bat, Come Under My Hat

Bat, bat, come under my hat,
And I'll give you a slice of bacon.
And when I bake,
I'll give you a cake,
If I am not mistaken.

Three Young Rats

Three young rats with black felt hats,
Three young ducks with white straw flats,
Three young dogs with curling tails,
Three young cats with demi-veils,
Went out to walk with two young pigs,
In satin vests and sorrel wigs,
But suddenly it chanced to rain,
And so they all went home again.

Rain, Rain, Go Away

Rain, rain, go away,
Come again another day,
Little Johnny wants to play.

Georgie Porgie

Georgie Porgie pudding and pie,
Kissed the girls and made them cry.
When the boys came out to play,
Georgie Porgie ran away.

Kookaburra

Kookaburra sits on an old gum tree,
Merry, merry king of the bush is he.
Laugh, kookaburra, laugh, kookaburra,
Gay your life must be.

Alouette

Alouette, gentille Alouette,
Alouette, je te plumerai.
Je te plumerai la tête,
Je te plumerai la tête,
Et la tête, et la tête,
Alouette, Alouette.

A Tisket, A Tasket

A tisket, a tasket,
A green and yellow basket.
I wrote a letter to my love,
But on the way I dropped it.
I dropped it, I dropped it,
And on the way I dropped it.
A little boy picked it up,
And put it in his pocket.

The Owl And The Pussycat

The owl and the pussycat went to sea,
In a beautiful pea-green boat.
They took some honey, and plenty of money,
Wrapped up in a five-pound note.

The owl looked up to the stars above,
And sang to a small guitar.
"O lovely pussy, O pussy my love,
What a beautiful pussy you are, you are!
What a beautiful pussy you are!"

Pussy said to the owl "You elegant fowl,
How charmingly sweet you sing!
Oh let us be married, too long we have tarried,
But what shall we do for a ring?"

Hickory, Dickory, Dare

Hickory, dickory, dare.
The pig flew up in the air.
The man in brown,
Soon brought him down,
Hickory, dickory, dare.

New Moon, True Moon

New moon, true moon,
True and bright,
If I have a true love,
Let me dream of him tonight!
If I am to marry rich,
Let me hear the cock crow!
If I am to marry poor,
Let me hear the hammer blow!

Little Nancy Etticoat

Little Nancy Etticoat,
With a white petticoat,
And a red nose.
She has no feet or hands,
The longer she stands,
The shorter she grows.

It's Raining, It's Pouring

It's raining, it's pouring,
The old man is snoring.
He went to bed,
And bumped his head,
And couldn't get up in the morning.

Wise Old Bird

A wise old owl lived in an oak.
The more he saw, the less he spoke.
The less he spoke, the more he heard.
Why can't we all be like that wise old bird?

Night-Light

You've no need to light a night-light,
On a light night like tonight,
For a night-light lights a slight light,
And tonight's a night that's light.

When a night's light, like tonight light,
It is really not quite right,
To light night-lights with their slight lights,
On a light night like tonight.

Someone Came Knocking

Someone came knocking at my wee small door,
Someone came knocking, I'm sure-sure-sure.
I listened, I opened, I looked to left and right,
But nought there was a-stirring in the still dark night.

Only the busy beetle tap-tapping in the wall,
Only from the forest the screech-owl's call,
Only the cricket whistling while the dew drops fall,
So I know not who came knocking, at all, at all, at all.

One Little Duck

One little duck,
He ran away,
Over the hill and far away.
Mother duck said,
"Quack, quack, quack, quack."
And the one little duck,
Came running back.

Once I Caught
A Fish Alive

One, two, three, four, five,
Once I caught a fish alive.
Six, seven, eight, nine, ten,
Then I let it go again.
Why did you let it go?
Because it bit my finger so.
Which finger did it bite?
This little finger on my right.

The Crocodile

If you should meet a crocodile,
Don't take a stick and poke him.
Ignore the welcome in his smile,
Be careful not to stroke him.

For as he sleeps upon the Nile,
He gets thinner and thinner,
So whenever you meet a crocodile,
He's ready for his dinner.

Row, Row, Row Your Boat

Row, row, row your boat,
Gently down the stream.
Merrily, merrily, merrily,
Life is but a dream.

Row, row, row your boat,
Gently down the stream.
If you see a crocodile,
Don't forget to scream.

Home On The Range

Home, home on the range,
Where the deer and the antelope play,
Where seldom is heard a discouraging word,
And the skies are not cloudy all day.

Playtime Fun

Jenny loved nothing more than when Ben came round to her house to play. As soon as his mother dropped him off, they would run and open Jenny's toy box and pull out all of her toys.

"We're going to have so much fun today," said Jenny, with a big smile.

First, Jenny let Ben choose which toys to play with. "I want to play with the toy cars," Ben said.

He put on a yellow hard hat and zoomed his digger along the floor, shouting "VROOOM!" Lining the digger up next to Jenny's red car, the two friends raced each other across the carpet.

Next, Jenny chose what game they would play. "Let's see who can be the noisiest," she said. Ben grabbed a toy drum and played it as fast as he could. Jenny giggled as she chattered loudly on her play telephone.

Soon, Ben's mom was at the door. It was time for Ben to go home. Jenny was sad but she knew that he would be back to play again soon. The friends gave each other a big hug goodbye.

"Playtime with you is always the best!" said Jenny, as she waved goodbye to Ben.

Deena's Dolly

Deena had lost her best dolly on holiday. When she came home, she played with Teddy and she played with Bunny, but it wasn't the same. None of her other toys were anywhere near as pretty, or as soft, or as much fun to play princesses with. Tears rolled down Deena's cheeks as she thought about her dolly, lost and all alone. "I want my best dolly back," cried Deena.

Mom gave Deena a lovely, soft cuddle. "Would you like to go next door and play with Cilla?" she asked. "That will cheer you up."

"Yes, please," said Deena and she wiped away her tears.

She knew that Cilla would think of lots of fun games for the two of them to play together. It would be nice to not think about her lost dolly for a little while.

At Cilla's house, Deena did some drawing and played on the swing. Then, Cilla's mom brought out the toy box. It was full of lovely toys.

"Look, here's my best dolly," said Cilla with a great, big smile. But, poor Deena didn't have a best dolly to play with anymore and she began to cry.

"Don't worry about not having a dolly, Deena," said Cilla's mommy, gently. "There are lots of pretty dollies here to play with." She got them out of the toy box. "Pick the one you like the most," she said, kindly.

Deena had a lovely time playing with the dollies. Cilla and her mommy were very kind because they let Deena keep the one she liked the best. "Thank you," said Deena. She was very happy. It felt lovely to have a new best dolly.

Charlie's Big Dig

It was a lovely summer day and Charlie and Roly were playing in their garden. They were lounging in the sun when suddenly they saw a furry head appear over the fence. A few seconds later, another one bounced up, too.

Charlie and Roly tried to jump up, to see who it was, but the fence was too high. No matter how hard they tried, they couldn't jump high enough to see what was happening on the other side of the fence.

"I want to find out who's bouncing next door," said Charlie. "Me, too," added Roly. So, they sniffed around at the bottom of the fence and then they began to dig.

Charlie dug a bit, then Roly dug a bit. Soon, there was a hole just big enough for Charlie to poke his head through. He wiggled into the hole, excited to see who was on the other side. But soon, Charlie found that he couldn't wiggle through anymore. He was stuck.

Luckily, his mother was watching from the kitchen window. "I knew you two would get up to mischief," she said, coming outside.

Mom dug and dug and soon, Charlie was free. "Next time, if you need help with something, remember to ask," she said, gently.

"Sorry," said Charlie. "Sorry," said Roly. Then they started to fill in the hole.

When the soil was all nice and smooth, Charlie's mother took him and Roly
next door to play. They had lots of fun, jumping and bouncing on the big
trampoline with their new friends, Daisy and Jane. Best of all, Mum was there
to make sure there was no more mischief.

The Lonley Owl

It was a clear, starlit, night and the moon smiled down on Owl's tree in the middle of the woods. But Owl wasn't feeling happy at all. Even the twinkling stars and glowing moonbeams couldn't cheer him up. Owl was feeling sad because he had nobody to play with. "Everyone else is asleep while I'm wide awake," sighed Owl. "It's just no fun being alone."

"I'll play with you," barked a voice from the bushes. Out trotted Fox. "Twit-twoo," hooted Owl. "I won't be alone because Fox wants to play." "Catch me if you can," called Fox, speeding off into the undergrowth.

Owl launched himself into the air to search for his new friend. But he couldn't catch up with super-fast Fox. At last, feeling tired, he flopped down to rest.

Just then, Mouse scurried by. Owl was so thrilled to see him, he swooped down at once. Before he could open his beak and ask Mouse to play, the terrified creature had run away. "Squeak!" said Mouse. "Owl looks like he wants to eat me for dinner tonight."

Now Owl was feeling really sad. No one wanted to play with him. Suddenly, he heard a beautiful chirping from up in the trees. The birds had come out to sing!

"It's too early for the dawn chorus," said Owl. "What are you all doing?"
"We saw what happened and thought you needed cheering up," cheeped Lark.
"Come and play with us."

The sun was peeking over the horizon, sending the first orange rays of daylight through the trees. Owl lifted up his beak and, joining in the sweet birdsong, he hooted in delight. "Twit-twoo," he hooted. I've got friends to keep me company after all."

Tania's Tutu

Tania wanted to look like a proper ballerina, so she rummaged in her dressing-up box. But Mom's old skirt was raggy and torn. The too-big ballet shoes were scuffed and worn.

"I don't look like a proper ballerina at all," said Tania. Then, two fat tears rolled down her cheeks.

Tania's mom saw how upset she was. So, she went into the attic and found her old sewing box. Tania was amazed when her mom lifted the box's lid. It was full of slinky silk, cloth buttons, beads and shiny pink ribbon. "We'll use all of this to make you a very special tutu," said Mom.

So, Mom stitched and sewed and Tania stuck on sequins.

At last, Tania's tutu was finished. It was pink and frilly and very sparkly. Tania looked in the mirror. "It's lovely. Thank you, Mommy," she said.

Then, Mom unwrapped the strangely shaped parcel. "These ballet shoes are too small for your cousin Lizzy," she said, "so she's given them to you." Tania was very happy. "I want to dance and dance," she said.

That afternoon, Tania danced in her lovely, new tutu. She pointed her toes, held up her arms and waved her hands. Then, she whirled and twirled until she finished with a very graceful bow.

Everyone clapped and cheered. "Well done, Tania," they said. "Now you really are a proper ballerina!"

Aladdin

Long ago, in a great city, there lived a poor, hungry orphan boy named Aladdin. He had no home of his own, so he had to live on the streets and steal food to survive.

One day, a wealthy-looking man called to Aladdin in the marketplace. Aladdin thought the man was about to punish him for stealing and he tried to hide. "Don't be afraid," said the man. "I am your long-lost uncle, Abenazer. If you will help me, Aladdin, together we will make our fortune."

Aladdin didn't know that Abenazer was not really his uncle, but a wicked magician. Abenazer wanted a magic lamp that lay in an enchanted cave nearby, but he was cowardly and wanted Aladdin to get it for him.

Abenazer took Aladdin to the cave entrance, which was a small hole that led down a steep slope. "You may take all the treasure you find inside," said Abenazer. "Just bring me the dirty old lamp from the middle of the cave."

Aladdin went into the cave. He had never seen so much treasure. Gold was piled in heaps on the floor and the walls of the cave were covered with precious stones. Aladdin filled his pockets with jewels and gold coins.

Aladdin found the old lamp on a large stone in the middle of the cave. He took the lamp, but the moment it was in his hands, the floor started to shake. Aladdin looked up to find the entrance to the cave closing above him. Climbing as fast as he could, he reached the opening of the cave. "Help me out, Uncle," cried Aladdin.

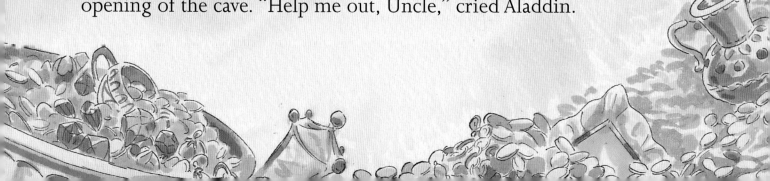

"Give me the lamp first," said Abenazer. He tried to grab the lamp, but he knocked Aladdin, who was still holding it, down the rocky slope.

Aladdin tumbled back down into the cave and when he looked up, the entrance to the cave had closed behind him.

Aladdin sat in the dark, wondering what to do. He was trapped in the cave. "That man was no uncle of mine," he said, rubbing the dirty lamp to clean it. "How I wish I had some light in here."

Suddenly, a mighty, green genie whooshed from the spout of the lamp. The genie made more lamps appear, so the cave was flooded with light.

"I am the genie of the lamp. My wish is your command. What is your next wish, Master?" said the genie.

Aladdin was amazed. "I wish I were at home," he said. The genie clicked his fingers and Aladdin was back in the marketplace, surrounded by the jewels he was carrying.

From then on, the genie appeared every time Aladdin rubbed the lamp. It could make all of Aladdin's wishes come true. "I wish for a great palace!" cried Aladdin. The ground shook and a mighty, marble palace rose from the desert. It was bigger than the palace of the sultan himself.

Soon, Aladdin was the richest man in the city. He married the sultan's daughter and they lived happily in their desert palace.

The Dancing Party

Louise loved to dance more than anything else in the world. She dreamed of dressing up in a pretty dancing outfit and twirling ribbons in time to music

Every day, she watched the children next door dancing and playing in their gardens. She wished that she could dance with them, instead of just watching from her bedroom window.

The problem was that Louise didn't think she fitted in with everyone else. She was very shy and she wasn't dainty like a dancer should be.

Louise felt so lonley and so sad, that she stood in front of her mirror and started to cry. Her mother didn't like to see her upset. Suddenly, she had an idea that she thought might cheer Louise up.

The next day, Louise's mother asked if she would like to walk around the garden. When they stepped outside, Louise saw the girls from next door playing there. "Hello," said one of them. "My name's Emma and this is my sister, Lucy. Your mum told us that you're a wonderful dancer!"

"Would you like to help us make up a new dance?" asked Lucy. "We're just trying out some new steps."

"Yes, of course," Louise replied with a big smile. In no time at all, the three girls were twirling around the garden in pretty hats and ribbons.
"You dance beautifully," Emma told Louise.

The three girls played together for the rest of the day. They had lots of fun and Louise was so happy to have made new friends. From then on, she never felt lonely again.

Billy and Cuddles

Billy and Cuddles loved nothing more than playing in the rain. From inside, they watched it split-splat and drip-drop down through the window. It looked wonderfully splashy and wet out there.

"Please Mother," Billy said. "Please can Cuddles and I go and splash about in the rain?"

"Yes," said Mother, "but both of you must put on your wellies
and your raincoats. Remember now, don't get too muddy or wet."

"Hurray!" shouted Cuddles and Billy. They put on their coats and wellies
as fast as they possibly could and ran outside to play in the rain.

When they got outside, the first thing that Cuddles and Billy did was jump in a huge, muddy puddle. They laughed as they splashed each other with the yucky, brown mud.

"Ugh!" said Cuddles after a little while of being covered in mud. "This stuff is horrible. How are we going to clean it off our coats?" Billy smiled, because he'd suddenly had a wonderful idea.

Billy ran towards a big puddle of water. "I know how we can get clean," he said to Cuddles. "By splashing each other even more in this big water puddle!"

Cuddles laughed and jumped in the puddle straight away. In no time at all, the mud was all gone from their coats and wellies. Playing in the rain might be mucky, but it was lots of fun, too!

Dinky's Great Escape

Josh and Amy were getting very worried. By accident, they had left their hamster Dinky's cage open and he had escaped. They looked everywhere for him, but they couldn't find where he was hiding.

They looked in the wardrobe and in all the drawers. They even looked under the bed, but Dinky was nowhere to be found. "Where could he be?" cried Josh.

Eventually, they decided to tell their mother. As always, she knew exactly what to do. "We'll have to search the entire house for Dinky," she said. "But we'll have to be very quiet, otherwise we'll scare him away from wherever he's hiding."

So, Josh, Amy and mother crept all over the house. They looked in every nook and cranny and dark corner and shadowy place. But Dinky was nowhere to be found.

Suddenly, their mother had a wonderful idea. "Quickly!" she said. "Go and get some of Dinky's hamster nuts."

So, Josh ran off to fetch them. When he came back, their mother crept, very carefully, across the landing and laid a trail of nuts all the way back to Josh and Amy's bedroom.

Soon, Dinky was safely back in his cage. Mother smiled at Amy and Josh.
"Off to bed, you two," she said. "And next time, remember to close Dinky's
door." Amy and Josh promised that they would. Then, they settled down for a
good night's sleep.

Fright Night

Jamie and his best friend, Connor, knew that they should never have stepped foot inside the spooky old house on the hill. "I dare you to go in," Connor had said to Jamie. "I bet it's haunted."

Now they were inside and the house was even spookier than they had imagined. Jamie noticed a pair of green eyes looking out from a dark alcove. "I just saw them move," he cried to Connor. "Quick, run!

The friends ran upstairs, far away from the scary green eyes. "Phew," said Connor, at the top of the stairs. "That was close."

Suddenly, two floaty, white things came flying towards Jamie and Connor's faces. "Argh!" they both screamed, running back down the stairs, as fast as they possibly could.

As they tried to catch their breath at the bottom of the stairs, Jamie heard a noise coming from the room next to them. He nervously pushed open the door.

There, miaowing happily in the middle of the room, was a silky, black cat. He had huge green eyes, which explained what the two friends had seen in the hallway. Behind him was a cupboard full of white shirts.

"It must have been the cat, flinging shirts at us down the stairs, too. Not ghosts chasing us," said Connor. The two friends left the house on the hill, giggling at how silly they had been.

Just as they started to walk away, Jamie suddenly spotted something on the top floor of the house. "Look," he gasped, pointing to the window. "Perhaps the house on the hill is pretty spooky after all!"

Well Done, Leonard

A stranger had come to live at Leonard's house. Mom said it was Leonard's baby brother and he was called Charlie. Dad said that Leonard was a big brother now and it was a very important job.

He looked a lot like Leonard, but he was very small. He was always wrapped up nice and warm in blankets, he drank lots of milk and sometimes he cried very loudly.

But Leonard didn't like being a big brother. Charlie couldn't talk, or run about, or play in the garden. In fact, he spent most of the time asleep. "Being a big brother is boring," said Leonard.

He thought that there was nothing fun about having Charlie living in the house with him. Dad said that if Leonard was patient, Charlie would be able to play games with him very soon.

One day, Mom was busy cleaning. The vacuum cleaner whirred and crackled and made a terrible racket. Charlie woke up and began to cry. Mom couldn't hear and Dad couldn't hear. But, Leonard could hear.

He ran into the living room and tugged at Mom's arm. "Charlie's crying," he said. So, Mom went to give Charlie a cuddle. "Well done, Leonard," she said. "Well done," said Dad. "You're a very good, big brother."

As a special treat, Mom and Dad took Leonard to the park. He slid down the slide and whirled around on the roundabout.

Leonard had so much fun playing in the park all day long. Best of all, he knew that when Charlie was older, they would be able to have fun at the park together.

"I can't wait for Charlie to be old enough to play with," said Leonard. "Being a big brother is the best thing ever."

Heather And The Weather

Heather enjoyed playing outside more than anything. She loved to run around the garden, playing on her swing-set and whooshing down the slide.

One day, Heather was sitting at the top of her slide, when she noticed the sky growing very dark. The sun disappeared behind a big, grey cloud. "I think it might rain," Heather told a little bird, who was already diving for cover.

That night, it rained and rained. Water fell down from the sky in huge blobs and splats. When Heather went outside to play in the morning, she wore her red wellington boots, her yellow rain coat and her flowery rain hat.

Before she had even moved from the front step, the rain hat leaked and Heather got all wet. She bravely walked out into the garden anyway.

The rain got much worse and soon it had turned into a storm. The lightening crackled and flashed. The thunder rumbled loudly and Heather got quite scared. "I wish I could splash in the puddles," said Heather to the little bird. "But it's too scary out here today!"

The next day, the thunder storm was over. The sun was shining brightly in the sky. It was such a lovely, warm day that Heather put on her swimming costume and played in the paddling pool.

"I love this weather," she said to her mother, as she splashed in her pool. "It's perfect for playing outside!"

Counting Sheep

"I'm still awake," called Sam for the third time that night.
"Try counting sheep," suggested his mother, with a yawn.
"But they're all fast asleep," Sam moaned.
"Not real sheep," laughed his mother, "Shut your eyes and imagine them."

Sam settled down in his cozy, little bed and tried his best to picture sheep.

It was no use. Every time Sam tried to picture sheep, another animal would come to mind. He imagined hens flapping over his bed. Sam tried to count them. "One, two, three…" he began.

The problem was, as each hen fluttered across, Sam imagined it letting out a loud squawk. "I'll never get to sleep with all this noise," said Sam. So, he stopped imagining hens and tried to think of something else.

Pigs had always seemed like nice animals to Sam, so he tried imagining them next. He snuggled down under his duvet and got ready to count.

But as the imaginary pigs trotted around his bed, Sam couldn't help imagining a terrible, mucky smell with them, too. "This isn't working," he spluttered, covering his nose.

Thinking about pigs obviously wasn't going to work. Cosy in his bed, Sam snuggled down and tried one last time to count sheep. "One, two, three…" he began.

This time, imagining sheep was easy. They weren't too noisy or smelly and before Sam had even counted to four, he had fallen fast asleep.

Garden Monsters

Outside, in the garden, Danny and Sam settled inside the old tent. They were camping in the garden for the first time ever. "This is exciting," they said. Then, they both sat and waited for night time to come.

Soon, the sun began to sink and shadows stretched, like long fingers, across the grass. Then, the sky grew dark and the night crept in.

"Brrr…" said Sam, shivering. "It's a bit chilly. Let's have some sandwiches and a drink." So, they tucked into their sandwiches and drank their juice.

Danny and Sam were just enjoying them when there was a rustling and a hooting noise outside. Then, something large flew past the tent.

"What was that?" asked Sam and he clicked on his torch. But there was nothing outside. So, they snuggled down into their soft, sleeping bags.

All was quiet for a while. Then, Danny saw something crawling up the tent. But, there wasn't just one thing – there were loads!

Suddenly, the tent flap flicked back. "I've just come to see if you are alright," said Dad.

"No! We aren't," said Danny and Sam. They told Dad all about the hooty noise and the creepy monsters. "The hooting was just the owl," said Dad. "The monsters are only garden snails. If you are worried, I can stay out here and keep you company."

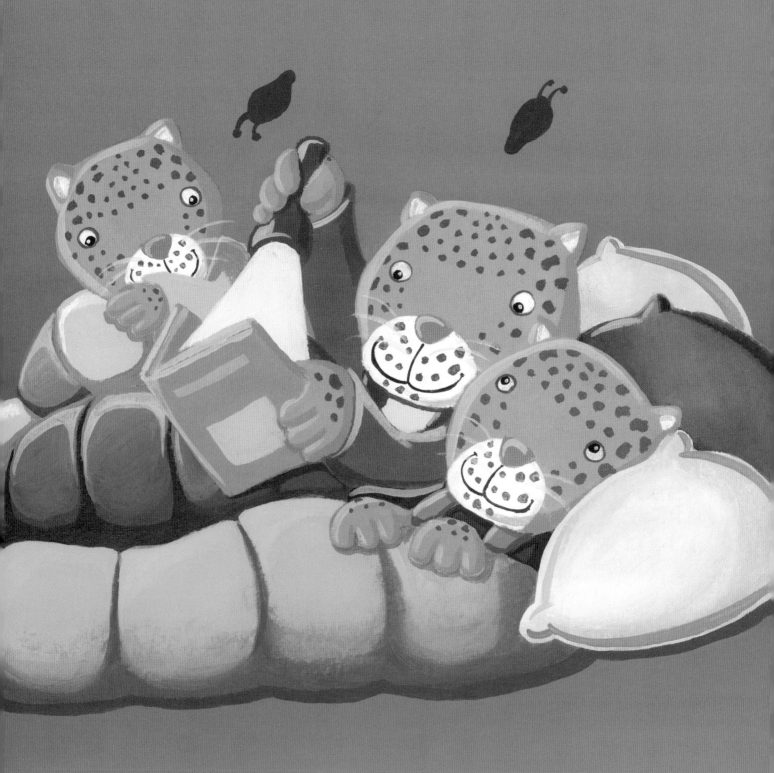

"Yes, please," said Danny and Sam. So, Dad got his sleeping bag and they all snuggled down. Then Dad told them stories by torchlight. Before long, everyone was cozy and warm. "Thank you, Dad," said Danny. "Thank you," said Sam. Now they felt like proper adventurers.

The Little, Blue Train

Everyone is waiting patiently on the station platform. Zebra, Hippo, Elephant and Giraffe have all got their bags packed. They can't wait to go on holiday!

The little, blue train pulls into the station with clickety wheels and a chimney that chugs.

"CHOO CHOO," the train goes, as the driver waves from the engine window. All aboard," cries the station master. The friends all climb on board the train. They find their seats and put their bags in the luggage racks, as the doors to the train are shut and locked. The station master blows sharply on his whistle and the little, blue train pulls away.

Zebra, Hippo, Elephant and Giraffe wave at all the sheep in the fields, as they chug through the countryside. "It's so exciting to be riding the train," says Elephant, with a big smile. The little, blue train chugs up a very steep hill, happy to be carrying lots of passengers.

Soon, the friends reach their stop. They all grab their bags and jump out onto the platform.

"Bye bye," they shout, as they all wave goodbye to the train driver. It's been a long day for the little, blue train. After a nice, long sleep, he'll be back again!

To Market

To market, to market, to buy a fat pig,
Home again, home again, jiggety jig.

To market, to market, to buy a fat hog,
Home again, home again, jiggety jog.

To market, to market, to buy a plum bun,
Home again, home again, market is done.

The Muffin Man

Oh, do you know the Muffin Man,
The Muffin Man,
The Muffin Man?
Do you know the Muffin Man,
That lives in Drury Lane?

Oh, yes I know the Muffin Man,
The Muffin Man,
The Muffin Man.
Yes l know the Muffin Man,
That lives in Drury Lane.

Hot-Cross Buns

Hot-cross buns, hot-cross buns!
One a-penny, two a-penny,
Hot-cross buns!

Dance To Your Daddy

Dance to your daddy,
My bonnie laddy,
Dance to your daddy,
My bonnie lamb.

You shall get a fishy,
In a little dishy,
You shall have a fishy,
When the boat comes in.

You shall get a coatie,
And a pair of breeches,
And you'll get an eggy,
And a bit of ham.

Here Is The Sea

Here is the sea,
The wavy sea,
Here is the boat,
And here is me!
All the fishes,
Down below,
Wiggle their tails,
And away they go!

The Big Ship Sails

The big ship sails,
On the alley, alley oh.
The alley, alley oh.
The big ship sails,
On the alley, alley oh.
On the last day of December.

The Pirate Ship

We're going this way, that way,
Forwards, backwards,
Over the deep blue sea.
A bottle of rum,
To warm my tum,
And that's the life for me.

Wash On Monday

Wash on Monday,
Iron on Tuesday,
Bake on Wednesday,
Brew on Thursday,
Churn on Friday,
Mend on Saturday,
Meeting on Sunday.

Warm Kitty

Soft kitty, warm kitty,
Little ball of fur.
Happy kitty, sleepy kitty.
Purr, purr, purr.

Pease Porridge

Pease porridge hot,
Pease porridge cold,
Pease porridge in the pot,
Nine days old.
Some like it hot,
Some like it cold,
Some like it in the pot,
Nine days old.

Pat-A-Cake

Pat-a-cake, pat-a-cake,
Baker's man.
Bake me a cake,
As fast as you can.
Roll it, and poke it,
And mark it with B.
And throw it in the oven,
For baby and me.

I'm a Dingly Dangly Scarecrow

I'm a dingly dangly scarecrow,
With a flippy floppy hat.
I can shake my hands like this,
I can shake my feet like that.

The North Wind Doth Blow

The north wind doth blow,
And we shall have snow,
And what will poor robin do then,
Poor thing?
He'll sit in a barn,
And keep himself warm,
And hide his head under his wing,
Poor thing!

My Shadow

I have a little shadow,
That goes in and out with me.
And what can be the use of him,
Is more than I can see.
He is very, very like me,
From the heels up to the head.
And I see him jump before me,
When I jump into my bed.

Miss Polly Had
A Dolly

Miss Polly had a dolly who sick, sick, sick,
So she called for the doctor to be quick, quick, quick.
The doctor came with his bag and his hat,
And he knocked on the door with a rat-a-tat-tat.

He looked at the dolly and he shook his head,
And he said, "Miss Polly, put her straight to bed!"
He wrote on a paper for a pill, pill, pill.
"I'll be back in the morning with the bill, bill, bill."

Roses Are Red

Roses are red,
Violets are blue,
Sugar is sweet,
And so are you!

See-Saw, Margery Daw

See-saw, Margery Daw,
Jacky shall have a new master.
He shall have but a penny a day,
Because he can't work any faster.

Ring-A-Ring O'Roses

Ring-a-ring o'roses,
A pocket full of posies,
Atishoo! Atishoo!
We all fall down.

This Little Piggy

This little piggy went to market,
This little piggy stayed at home,
This little piggy had roast beef,
This little piggy had none.
And this little piggy went...
"Wee wee wee," all the way home.

Tom, Tom, The Piper's Son

Tom, Tom, the piper's son,
Stole a pig and away he ran.
The pig was eat,
And Tom was beat,
And Tom went howling down the street.

Barber, Barber

Barber, barber, shave a pig!
How many hairs to make a wig?
Four and twenty, that's enough!
Give the barber a pinch of snuff.

Gregory Griggs

Gregory Griggs,
Gregory Griggs,
Had forty-seven,
Different wigs.

He wore them up,
He wore them down,
To please the people,
Of Boston town.

He wore them east,
He wore them west,
But he could never tell,
Which he loved best.

Aiken Drum

There was a man lived in the moon,
Lived in the moon, lived in the moon.
There was a man lived in the moon,
And his name was Aiken Drum.

And his hat was made of good cream cheese,
Of good cream cheese, of good cream cheese.
And his hat was made of good cream cheese,
And his name was Aiken Drum.

And he played upon a ladle, a ladle, a ladle,
And he played upon a ladle.
And his name was Aiken Drum.

Puff The Magic Dragon

Puff the Magic Dragon lived by the sea,
And frolicked in the autum mist,
In a land call Honelee.
Little Jackie Paper loved that rascal Puff,
And brought him strings and sealing wax,
And other fancy stuff.

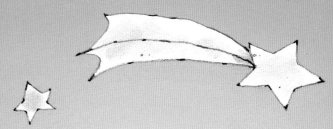

Three Little Men

Three little men in a fllying saucer,
Flew around the Earth one day.
They looked left and right,
But didn't like the sight,
So one man flew away.

Two Little Men

Two little men in a flying saucer,
Flew around the Earth one day.
They looked left and right,
But didn't like the sight,
So one man flew away.

One Little Man

One little man in a flying suacer,
Flew around the Earth one day.
He looked all around and saw a town,
And said, "Well I might just stay!"

Oh, My Darling

Oh, my darling, oh, my darling,
Oh, my darling Clementine,
You are lost and gone forever,
Dreadful sorry, Clementine.

Up In The Green Orchard

Up in the green orchard,
There is a green tree.
The finest of pippins,
That you may see.
The apples are ripe,
And ready to fall,
And Robin and Richard,
Shall gather them all.

Blow Wind, Blow

Blow wind, blow! And go mill, go!
That the miller may grind his corn.
That the baker may take it,
And into bread make it,
And bring us a loaf in the morn.

A Windmill In Old Amsterdam

A mouse lived in a windmill in old Amsterdam,
A windmill with a mouse in, and he wasn't grousing,
He sang every morning, "How lucky I am,
Living in a windmill in old Amsterdam!"

A Duck And A Drake

A duck and a drake,
And a nice barley cake,
With a penny to pay the old baker.
A hop and a scotch,
Is another notch,
Slitherum, slatherum, take her.

Where Are You Going, My Pretty Maid?

"Where are you going, my pretty maid?"
"I'm going a-milking, sir," she said.
"May I go with you, my pretty maid?"
"You're kindly welcome, sir," she said.
"What is your father, my pretty maid?"
"My father's a farmer, sir," she said.

Betty Botter

Betty Botter bought some butter,
"But," she said, "This butter's bitter,
If I put it in my batter,
It will make my batter bitter;
But a bit of better butter,
Will but make bitter batter better."
So she bought a bit of better butter,
And made her bitter batter better.

Skip To My Lou

Skip, skip, skip to my Lou,
Skip, skip, skip to my Lou,
Skip, skip, skip to my Lou,
Skip to my Lou, my darlin'.

Going To St. Ives

As I was going to St. Ives, I met a man with seven wives.
Each wife had seven sacks, each sack had seven cats,
Each cat had seven kittens: kittens, cats, sacks and wives.
How many were going to St. Ives?

Pretty Maid

Pretty maid, pretty maid,
Where have you been?
Gathering a posie,
To give to the Queen.

Pretty maid, pretty maid,
What gave she you?
She gave me a diamond,
As big as my shoe.

Old King Cole

Old King Cole,
Was a merry old soul,
And a merry old soul was he.

He called for his pipe,
And he called for his bowl,
And he called for his fiddlers three!

A Tudor

A tudor who tooted a flute,
Tried to tutor two tooters to toot.
Said the two to their tutor,
"Is it harder to toot,
Or to tutor two tooters to toot?"

The Queen Of Hearts

The Queen of Hearts,
She made some tarts,
All on a summer's day.

The Knave of Hearts,
He stole those tarts,
And took them clean away.

The King of Hearts,
Called for the tarts,
And beat the Knave full sore.

The Knave of Hearts,
Brought back the tarts,
And vowed he'd steal no more.

Red Sky At Night

Red sky at night,
Shepherd's delight.
Red sky in the morning,
Shepherd's warning.

She'll Be Comin' 'Round The Mountain

She'll be coming 'round the mountain when she comes,
She'll be coming 'round the mountain when she comes,
She'll be coming 'round the mountain, coming 'round the mountain,
She'll be coming 'round the mountain when she comes.

The Bear Went Over The Mountain

The bear went over the mountain,
The bear went over the mountain,
The bear went over the mountain,
To see what he could see.

And all that he could see,
Was the other side of the mountain,
The other side of the mountain,
The other side of the mountain,
Was all that he could see.

Three Little Bears

Three little bears,
Deciding what to do,
One fell asleep,
Then there were two!

Two little bears,
Having lots of fun,
One went home,
Then there was one!

One little bear,
Feeling all alone,
Ran to his mother,
Then there were none!

Butterfly, Butterfly

Butterfly, butterfly, flutter around.
Butterfly, butterfly, touch the ground.
Butterfly, butterfly, fly so free.
Butterfly, butterfly, land on me!
Butterfly, butterfly, reach the sky,
Butterfly, butterfly, say good-bye!

Lucy Locket

Lucy Locket lost her pocket,
Kitty Fisher found it.
Not a penny was there in it,
Only ribbon round it.

Miss Mary Mack

Miss Mary Mack, Mack, Mack,
All dressed in black, black, black,
With silver buttons, buttons, buttons,
All down her back, back, back.

The Little Girl

There was a little girl who had a little curl,
Right in the middle of her forehead.
When she was good, she was very, very good,
But when she was bad, she was horrid.

Draw A Pail Of Water

Draw a pail of water,
For my lady's daughter.
Her father's a king and her mother's a queen,
Her two little sisters are dressed in green,
Stamping grass and parsley,
Marigold-leaves and daises,
One rush, two rush!
Pray thee, fine lady, come under my bush.

Pussycat, Pussycat

Pussycat, pussycat, where have you been?
I've been to London to visit the Queen.
Pussycat, pussycat, what did you do there?
I frightened a little mouse under her chair.

The King Of France

The King of France went up the hill,
With twenty thousand men.
The King of France came down the hill,
And never went up again.

Brother John

Are you sleeping? Are you sleeping?
Brother John, Brother John,
Morning bells are ringing,
Morning bells are ringing.
Ding, dang, dong. Ding, dang, dong.

I Love Little Kitty

I love little kitty, her coat is so warm,
And if I am kind, she'll do me no harm.
So I'll not pull her tail, nor drive her away,
But kitty and I very gently will play.
I'll sit by the fire, and give her some food,
And Kitty will love me because I am good.

Hush-A-Bye

Hush-a-bye, baby, on the tree top,
When the wind blows the cradle will rock,
When the bough breaks the cradle will fall,
Down will come baby, bough, cradle and all.

The Apple Tree

Here is the tree with leaves so green,
Here are the apples that hang between.
When the wind blows, the apples fall,
Here is a basket to gather them all.

A Swarm Of Bees

A swarm of bees in May,
Is worth a load of hay.
A swarm of bees in June,
Is worth a silver spoon.
A swarm of bees in July,
Is not worth a fly.

Miss Muffet

Little Miss Muffet,
Sat on a tuffet,
Eating her curds and whey.
There came a big spider,
And sat down beside her,
And frightened Miss Muffet away.

This Is The Sun

This is the sun,
So big and round.
This is a seed,
So snug in the ground.
These are the flowers,
That wave in the breeze.
These are the yachts,
That sail on the seas.

There Was A Little Turtle

There was a little turtle,
Who lived in a box.
He swam in puddles,
And climbed on rocks.
He snapped at the mosquito,
He snapped at the flea,
He snapped at the minnow,
And he snapped at me.
He caught the mosquito,
He caught the flea,
He caught the minnow,
But he didn't catch me!

Three Wise Men

Three wise men of Gotham,
Went to sea in a bowl.
If the bowl had been stronger,
My song would have been longer.

If All The World Were Paper

If all the world were paper,
And all the sea were glue,
If all the sky were cherry pie,
Whatever would we do?

Have You Ever

Have you ever, ever, ever, in your long-legged life,
Met a long-legged sailor with a long-legged wife?
No, I never, never, never, in my long-legged life,
Met a long-legged sailor with a long-legged wife.

Bedtime Frogs

It was nearly bedtime in the little frogs' house. They were still running around and playing games when Mother Frog came over, looking at her watch.

"Hop upstairs, little ones," said Mother Frog. "Brush your teeth and put on your pajamas. It's time for you all to go to sleep."

The little frogs didn't want to go to bed yet though. "I've got a sore throat," croaked one. "Me, too!" croaked another.

Soon all four little frogs were gathered around their mother, complaining that their throats were sore. They cried and they wailed and the wouldn't get into bed.

Mother Frog knew that she had to do something to get her little frogs to go to sleep.

Mother Frog knew the best cure for a sore throat was the special medicine that she kept in a secret cupboard.

She fetched the medicine and poured it into a spoon. Mother Frog's medicine was drippy, gloopy and runny. Each little frog had a spoonful and it slid right down into their tummies.

Soon, all four little frogs were tucked up in their beds. Mother Frog read them a bedtime story and kissed each of them goodnight.

The little frogs all felt much better after their medicine and none of them complained about their throats.

Mother Frog turned out the light, as all four little frogs fell fast asleep.

The Three Billy Goats Gruff

Once upon a time, Three Billy Goats Gruff saw a far-away meadow. It was full of young, fresh, green grass that looked delicious. But the meadow was on the other side of a rushing river. "I am going to cross the bridge and try that delicious grass," said the youngest Billy Goat Gruff.

He skipped along to the bridge and started to cross it. His little hooves went trip-trap, trip-trap on the bridge. Suddenly, a voice came from under the bridge. It was a snarling, slobbering, snickering kind of voice. "Who's that trip-trapping over my bridge?" it said.

It was a hideous troll. He leapt out from under the bridge and cried, "I'm going to gobble you up for my dinner!" He sharpened his claws and got ready to leap on the smallest Billy Goat Gruff.

The little Billy Goat Gruff was frightened, but he thought quickly. Before the troll could leap on him, he cried, "Wait! Don't eat me! I am very thin and small. If you let me eat the grass on the other side of the bridge, I will grow big and fat. Then you can eat me when I come back."

The troll was hungry, but he was greedy, too and not very clever. "All right, little goat," said the troll. "I'll let you go, but make sure you're fattened up when you come back." So, the smallest Billy Goat Gruff trip-trapped all the way across the bridge.

Soon, the middle-sized Billy Goat Gruff said to the biggest goat, "I am worried about our brother. I am going across the bridge to see if he is safe." He went to the bridge and started to cross it. The middle-sized goat's hooves were heavier than the smallest goat's and they made a heavier trip-trap, trip-trap sound on the bridge once again, as he crossed.

"Who's that trip-traping over my bridge?" he said. "A bigger billy goat, eh? I'm going to gobble you up for my diner!"

"Wait," called the middle-sized Billy Goat Gruff. "I may be bigger than my brother, but if I eat the grass on the other side of the bridge, I'll grow fatter still." The troll agreed again, even though by now he was hungrier than ever.

It wasn't long before the biggest Billy Goat Gruff followed his two brothers. He went to the bridge and started to cross it. The biggest Billy Goat Gruff was heavy and his hooves went TRIP-TRAP, TRIP-TRAP on the bridge.

The troll called out "Who's that trip-trapping across my bridge? Whoever you are, I'll gobble you up for my dinner." He leapt onto the bridge, but stopped suddenly when he saw who was walking across. The biggest Billy Goat Gruff was enormous. and he had gigantic, curved horns.

Now it was the troll's turn to be afraid. The biggest Billy Goat Gruff was even bigger than he was. The troll hesitated for a moment, but then he remembered how hungry he was. He leapt at the big goat, but the biggest Billy Goat Gruff ran at the troll and butted him hard.

The troll flew off the bridge and into the fast-running stream. The stream carried the troll far away, down the mountain and he was never seen again. The three Billy Goats Gruff ate all the grass they wanted and became very fat and they lived happily ever after in their lush, green meadow.

The Magic Unicorn

More than anything in the world, Sarah wanted her own pony. She had pictures of ponies all over her walls, but she knew that her family couldn't afford to buy her one.

One sunny day, Sarah was sitting in her room when she heard a strange noise. She looked out of her window and saw a beautiful, sparkling unicorn standing under the apple tree. She ran downstairs as quickly as she could.

"You appeared as if by magic," Sarah giggled, stroking the unicorn's nose. "I'll call you Magic!"

Sarah climbed onto Magic's back. The unicorn walked forward gracefully, then he started trotting, then cantering. Suddenly and incredibly, he lifted off the ground! Before long they were flying, far above the clouds, to a magical land.

When Sarah and Magic landed, fairies fluttered all around them, saying, "Welcome to Fairyland!" Sarah could see that they had arrived just as a party was about to begin.

There were lemonade fountains, delicous sandwiches, yummy cookies and lots of lovely fairy cakes. It was a real fairy feast. There was a bouncy castle, swings and a slide, too. Sarah had a wonderful time eating the party food and was even given her very own magic wand.

Soon, the party was over and it was time to leave Fairyland. Sarah thanked all the fairies and climbed onto Magic's back. They flew up into the sky again and Sarah laughed, as Magic swooped through the clouds. Finally, they landed back in Sarah's garden.

"I've had an amazing time," said Sarah as she stroked Magic's nose. "Please come back." Magic neighed as he flew away, and Sarah knew that their adventures had only just begun.

Princess Pirate

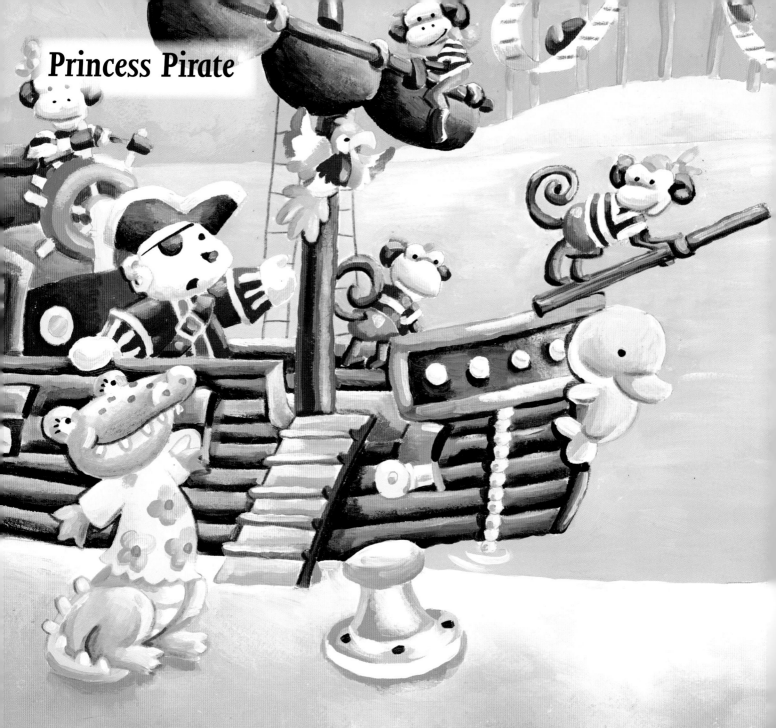

Once upon a time, there was a princess named Amber, who longed to be a pirate and have adventures on the Seven Seas. One day, she changed out of her princess clothes and sneaked away from her castle. She found an enormous, black pirate ship ship ready to set sail from harbor.

The captain saw Amber looking at the ship. "All aboard the Jolly Dolphin," he shouted. "Captain Crossbone is my name and I'm sailing for Treasure Island today. Will you join me, young lady?"

Captain Crossbone gave Amber a proper pirate hat and boots. She even had her own special sword. "That's for fighting bad pirates," he winked.

Suddenly, someone called out, "Land ahoy."
"It's Treasure Island," said the captain. "Ssh, be quiet now, we have to creep ashore, in case the treasure thieves are looking to plunder our loot. They're a fearsome bunch, make no mistake."

In no time at all, Captain Crossbone and Amber had found the treasure. They were taking it back to the ship, when suddenly, firece-looking, raggedy pirates ran out from the rocks. "Give us the treasure!" they cried, waving their swords in the air.

"Quick, take the treasure and run for the ship!" cried Captain Crossbone. So, Amber grabbed handfuls of jewels and glittering gems. She ran as fast as she could, out of the cave and over the sand, with the nasty pirates hot on her heels.

After a lot of sploshing and splashing, the treasure was safely on board.
"You're a very brave pirate princess," said Captain Crossbone to Amber.
"I recognised you as soon as I saw you, Princess Amber. I've known who
you are all along! You're welcome aboard the Jolly Dolphin any time you like."

The crew of the Jolly Dolphin agreed and they cheered. Then Captain
Crossbone bellowed, "Cast off, steady as she goes, it's time to head home."

Space Race

The most exciting place in the world for Jack and Josh was the Space Lab. Their dad worked there and today they were allowed to visit. As Jack and Josh arrived, a rocket whooshed from a launch pad.

"Wow!" cried Josh, as he walked behind his dad, "That's amazing!" "Wouldn't it be cool if we could be real astronauts?" said Jack, as he followed his little brother and their dad inside.

Dad said he was busy and disappeared into a laboratory. Jack looked around and pointed at a door that said: 'ROCKET TESTING. DO NOT ENTER.' He grinned at his brother and opened the door.

Inside was an incredible rocket. Jack climbed into it. "I wonder what this does?" he asked. Then, he pressed a big, green button. "No, don't!" cried Josh, but it was too late. There was a deep rumble. The rocket engines had started.

The two brothers were soon zooming through space, past asteroids and pink planets. "Let's explore that purple planet over there!" cried Jack, hitting a button that said 'LAND'. Once they had landed, the brothers put on space suits and stepped outside.

The purple planet was covered with weird, blue plants. "These are cool," said Josh. Suddenly, a long, blue tentacle reached out and grabbed his arm.

"An alien," shrieked Josh. "Help, it's got me!" Jack quickly wrestled the alien arm off of his brother. Together, they ran as fast as they could back to the rocket.

The brothers got inside and slammed the doors to the rocket quickly. Behind them, the angry creatures stretched out their tentacles. Josh hit the 'TAKE OFF' button and there was a great roar as the rocket blasted off.

The rocket hurtled through space, all the way back to Earth.
Josh pressed the 'LAND' button and they were soon safely back in the Space Lab.
Amazingly, no one had even noticed they had gone.

Outside, Dad was looking for them. "There you are," he said. "Have you had
an exciting time?"
"Oh, yes," said Josh, smiling at Jack. "It's been out of this world!"

Bubbles Learns To Swim

Bubbles wanted to swim with his friends, but, every time he tried, he just kept sinking and blowing big, watery bubbles. "I don't like swimming," he said, splashing about in his spotty armbands.

"Swish your arms and kick your legs, like me," said Dad. But when Bubbles tried, water shot up his nose and into his ears. "I hate swimming," he spluttered.

Bubbles felt very sad that he couldn't swim around the pool like everyone else. He wondered if there was something wrong with him. Maybe he would never be able to splash happily in the pool, or zoom down the big, yellow water slide. With tears in his eyes, Bubbles climbed out of the swimming pool.

Everyone else had a lovely time swimming in the pool. Alex and Sammy were whizzing down the waterslide. "Come on, Bubbles," they said. "It's great fun."

"Bubbles felt very cross. "Swimming is rubbish," he shouted, kicking his legs and swishing his arms, angrily. Then suddenly, Bubbles began to move.

"Bubbles, you're swimming!" cried Dad. "Keep going."

Soon, Bubbles was able to swim right across to his friends. "Well done, Bubbles!" they cried.

It wasn't long before Bubbles was having fun on the waterslide, too. "Yippee!" he cried, as he went, SPLASH! into the water, "I love swimming!"

The Last Teddy Bear

Elsie and Tom both wanted a new teddy bear. Their mothers had taken them both to the toy shop, but there was only one teddy bear left.

The last little teddy bear was sitting all on his own. He wore a bright blue jacket with red, patterned trousers, a little felt hat and small, furry boots. "He's lovely," said Elsie. She wanted to give him a huge cuddle. "He's so cute," said Tom.

They looked at their Mums and they looked at the little teddy. Then, at the same time, Tom and Elsie both said, "I want this one!" Elsie took one arm and Tom took the other and they both began to pull.
"He's mine," said Tom.
"No, he's mine," said Elsie. They pulled the teddy this way and that.

Tom toppled backwards and fell on the floor and Elsie landed with a bump, on her bottom. "Ouch!" they both said, looking very surprised. Their mothers looked very surprised, too. "It's not nice to squabble," they said.

"I want him!" said Elsie and she pulled at the little teddy's hat.
"No, I want him!" said Tom and he tugged at the teddy's boot.

Just then, the shop assistant came over holding another teddy, just like the other one. "Here you are," she said. "There's no need to argue. Now you can have a brand new teddy bear each."

Elsie and Tom felt very silly for squabbling. But, they were both very glad that they had new teddies to cuddle.

The Magic Present

Tom and Tia's uncle had bought them a present each. "They're cushions, but they've got a magical secret," he had said to them, when they tore the wrapping paper off.

The twins went upstairs and sat on their cushions. "What strange presents," said Tom. "I can't see anything special about them." Then, something amazing happened. Suddenly, each cushion began to move.

The cushions whooshed out of the window and across the garden. Tom and Tia whizzed over treetops and through the clouds. "Wow!" cried Tom. "Uncle's bought us magical flying cushions!"

They floated over a lush meadow with a sparkling stream running through it. The twins landed in the meadow and played there for the rest of the day.

"I'm tired," yawned Tia eventually. "I think it's time for us to go home." Tom agreed. "Please take us home, magic cushions," they pleaded.

As soon as they had spoken, the cushions whizzed around and shot off into the sky. Before they knew it, the twins were back in their bedroom and someone was knocking on the door.

"Come in," they called and their uncle appeared in the doorway. "Well," he laughed, "what do you think of your special presents?"

The twins looked at each other and smiled. All at once, they rushed across the room to give their uncle a big hug.

"They're certainly not boring," said Tom.
"Best present ever," agreed Tia.
"They're magic!" the twins shouted together.

Noah's Adventure

Noah the dolphin was playing hide-and-seek amongst the coral with his best friend, Sophie the shark.

"5...4...3...2...1... coming!" said Noah and he flicked his tail and went to look for his friend. Noah searched all over, amongst the swishy seaweed and the bright coral, but he couldn't find Sophie anywhere.

Suddenly, there was a noise from behind a rock. "Found you, Sophie!" cried Noah, poking his head round. But, it wasn't Sophie, it was a beady-eyed crab who snapped, angrily, with his giant claws. "Oh, no!" said Noah and he swam away, as fast as he could.

Just then, a swimming shoal of silvery fish dashed past. "Hello," said Noah, "Have you seen my friend, Sophie?" But the shoal shot off.

"Wait for me!" he cried, as he saw the fish disappear into a big, dark shipreck that sat on the bottom of the sea.

Noah swam into the shipwreck and started to explore. A cross-looking octopus came out of the shadows, waving his legs this way and that. "What are you doing here?" he asked. "This is my ship and it belongs to me. Go away."

Then, the unfriendly octopus waved his long, wiggly legs to shoo poor Noah away.

Suddenly, deep in the shipwreck, something else moved.

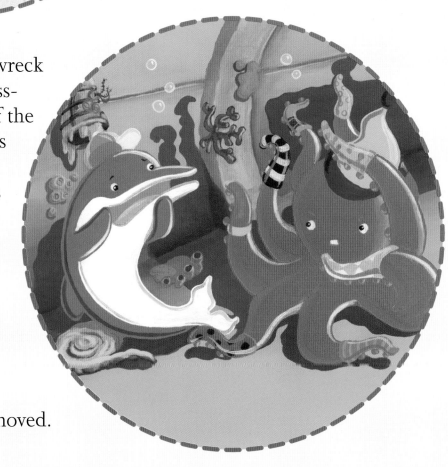

"Excuse me," said a voice. "This shipwreck belongs to everybody."
It was Noah's friend, Sophie. She had been hiding in the shipwreck all the
time. When the octopus saw how big she was, he swam off without
another word.

Noah was very happy to see his friend. "Come on, Noah," said Sophie. "Let's
go and play at home." Noah was very relieved. He loved playing hide-and-seek,
but he'd definitely had enough excitement for one day!

Rapunzel

Once upon a time, a poor couple lived next door to an enchantress. The enchantress had a garden full of fruit and vegetables.

Every year, all the delicious carrots, lettuces and apples lay on the ground and rotted. Meanwhile, the poor couple had hardly enough to eat.

One day, the poor man's wife was very hungry indeed. She was about to have a baby and needed to eat some food. Her husband climbed the wall and went into the enchantress' garden. He picked a big lettuce and took some juicy apples and carrots home to his wife. The man and his wife ate the food and it was delicious.

But the enchantress was very angry with the poor couple. "You have stolen from me," she said. "When your baby is born, I will take it from you." And sure enough, when a baby girl was born to the poor man and his wife, the wicked enchantress took her away.

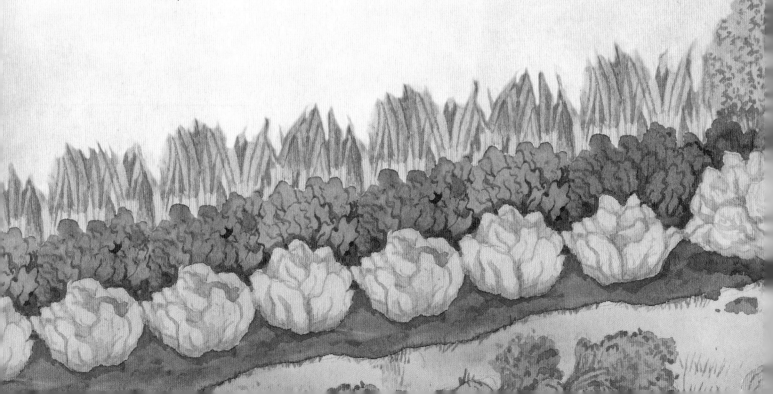

The girl was named Rapunzel and she grew into a young woman with very long, golden hair. The enchantress kept her imprisoned in a tall tower. She would stand on the ground and call out "Rapunzel, Rapunzel, let down your hair." Then Rapunzel would unpin her long, golden hair and lower it out of the window, so the enchantress could climb up into the tall tower.

One morning, a prince was wandering through the forest and saw the enchantress call out to Rapunzel, then climb up the golden locks. When the enchantress had left, the prince called out, "Rapunzel, Rapunzel, let down your hair."

Thinking the enchantress had returned, Rapunzel shook her hair out of the window, and the prince climbed up. Rapunzel was very surprised to see a handsome prince, instead of the enchantress. Rapunzel and the prince fell in love and the prince vowed to rescue her.

But the enchantress was clever. She saw that Rapunzel was happy and wanted to know why. So one day, she left the tower and hid nearby, watching to see what Rapunzel would do. She saw the prince arrive and realised that Rapunzel was in love with him.

Later, when the prince was gone, the enchantress returned to the tower. She grabbed her scissors and cut off Rapunzel's long golden hair. Then she muttered a spell and Rapunzel found herself far from the tower, in an unknown land, with no way to reach her prince.

Meanwhile, the enchantress waited in the tower for the prince to arrive. That night, he called out softly, "Rapunzel, Rapunzel, let down your hair." The enchantress lowered Rapunzel's hair. The prince climbed up to find the furious enchantress waiting for him. "So, you're the one who tried to steal my Rapunzel, are you?" she sneered.

The prince tried to grab the enchantress, but she pushed him backwards and he toppled out of the window, pulling Rapunzel's hair down with him. The prince landed in some bushes at the foot of the tower. He looked up at the enchantress who was shaking her fist and screaming with rage. She was alone in the tower and her spell could not be undone. The evil enchantress was trapped by her own magic.

The prince set off to look for Rapunzel. He wandered far and wide, searching towns and villages along the way. The prince had often heard people talk of a girl with beautiful golden hair, but no matter how hard he looked, he could never find Rapunzel.

One day, when the prince had almost given up hope, he heard a sweet voice singing. It was Rapunzel. She had found work on a farm and was singing sadly as she carried water from the well. The prince ran to Rapunzel and they embraced.

The prince took Rapunzel home to see her parents. They were overjoyed at the return of their daughter. Soon after, the prince married Rapunzel and they lived happily ever after. As for the enchantress, she was trapped in the tower for the rest of her days and never troubled anyone, ever again.

Seaside Rescue

Joy and Lulu were so happy to be spending the day at the beach. They loved to build sandcastles and splash in the waves. The two friends were having great fun collecting shells and pretty stones in their buckets, when suddenly they both heard a strange noise.

"It sounds like it's coming from this cave," said Joy, already running inside. "Come on, Lulu, let's investigate!"

As their eyes got used to the dark, the two friends looked around the cave. They couldn't see anyone hiding inside.

Then they heard a strange noise again, this time much louder.

"Look!" said Lulu. "There's a tail sticking out from behind that rock. Maybe something is stuck!"

Together, Lulu and Joy pushed the big rock out of the way. Sure enough, they found a baby seal sitting behind it.

The seal looked up at them with huge blue eyes. "He's so cute," said Joy.

"I wonder how long he's been stuck here all alone," said Lulu, looking at the seal sadly.

The two friends decided to take the baby seal back to the sea, where he belonged. The tide had started to come in, so they had to be quick.

Joy and Lulu picked up the baby seal and, as the waves lapped around their ankles, carried him out of the cave. Gently, they put the baby seal in the ocean.

Lulu and Joy held their breath, as the tiny seal bobbed up and down in the waves. Suddenly, he started swimming! The two friends then spotted a bigger seal swimming towards him. "It's his mother," cried Joy.

The girls smiled a one another as the big seal nuzzled her baby, welcoming him back. It had been the best day at the beach ever.

Uncle Percy's Potions

Jake and Emily were visiting their Uncle Percy, who lived in a big, old house. Uncle Percy always said that they were allowed to go anywhere in the house, except the basement. Curious to see what was down there, Jake and Emily sneaked away from their parents and to explore it.

"Maybe there's a secret laboratory, where Uncle Percy makes special potions," Jake said. He pushed the door that led to the basement and clicked his pocket torch on. Emily kept close to him as they crept down the winding stone steps.

At the bottom, the pale beam of light fell on shelves stacked with bottles full of different-colored liquids. "What are they?" asked Emily. "I think they're tspecial potions!" gasped Jake.

Suddenly, there was a sort of thumping and clumping coming along the corridor. Then, with a creak, the little door opened and feet shuffled slowly down the steep, stone steps.

"Quick, hide!" said Jake and he pulled Emily behind a dusty, old chest. The feet at the bottom of the steps clumped around the room.

"Hmm…" said a gruff voice. "Now, which of my special bottles shall I choose tonight?"

"It's Uncle Percy," whispered Jake. "I told you he was a mad professor!"

When Uncle Percy left, Jake and Emily found another doorway that led out of the basement. They barged through into a room where their mother, father and Uncle Percy were all sipping potions. "Don't drink that. It's a special potion and Uncle Percy's a mad professor!" shouted Jake.

Jake and Emily's parents and Uncle Percy looked at each other. They looked at Jake. Then, they burst out laughing.

"I suppose you could call my famous blueberry cordial a special potion," Chuckled Uncle Percy. "I make lots of flavors, too. Would you like to try one?"

Jake and Emily felt really silly. They said sorry to Uncle Percy for thinking he was a mad professor and had a delcious drink of tangy, raspberry cordial. Then they tasted the peach flavor and the lemon and blackberry, too. Discovering Uncle Percy's potions was the best thing ever.

The Winning Team

The whistle blew to start the finals of the Animal Football League. Smalltown United were playing Ripton Rovers, but the Smalltown players were nervous. They'd never beaten Ripton before.

"Come on," cried Smalltown's star player, Ryan. "We've got to try. Let's give it a go!" He dashed forward as a Ripton player kicked the ball, then with one big leap he jumped up to head it.

Ryan's header was fantastic, but as the game went on, things started to go badly for Smalltown. Joey dashed in to kick the ball, but was trampled into the mud by the bigger Ripton players. Ripton were squashing Smalltown's defence, and they couldn't do a thing about it.

The whistle finally blew for half time. Somehow, Ripton still hadn't scored, but they were by far the stronger team. "We've not got a chance in the second half," the Smalltown players all said to each other, sadly.

As the Smalltown players slouched into the dressing room, they felt very sad. Ryan wanted to give them all a great half time talk. "Don't give up!" he said. "There's still everything to play for."

"They're so much bigger than us, though," said Bobby. Ryan had an idea. "We've just need to play to our strengths," he said. "They might be bigger than us, but we can use that against them!" The other Smalltown players cheered. Ryan was right. They could still win the match.

The Ripton players took control of the ball, but this time the Smalltown
players were ready for them. They passed quickly to one another and finally,
Joey raced forward. Even though the Ripton players tried to stop him, he saw a
tiny gap between them. Joey was so fast, the Ripton keeper never even saw him
coming. "Goal!" shouted the referee.

The final whistle blew and the crowd roared. Smalltown had won!
At last, they were proud to be the winning team.

The Shiny Red Shoes

Angelina was very excited. She was going to a party at Pippa's house. "Do you want to wear your shiny, red shoes?" asked her mother. "They'll match your dress."

"No, thank you," said Angelina. "I'm going to wear my blue shoes."

"But you wear your blue shoes every day," said her mother. "The red ones will look much nicer."

"No, thank you," said Angelina, stubbornly. She was determined to wear her blue shoes to the party..

At Pippa's house, Angelina waved to her friend, Sarah. She had a lovely, yellow party dress on and shiny shoes to match.

Angelina looked down at her blue shoes, feeling a little sad. She wore the blue shoes to school every day, as well as wearing them to play outside in the garden and the park. They were very scruffy and they didn't match her red dress at all.

Then, Tommy came running over to say hello. He had his best jeans on and lovely, new trainers. Angelina looked down at her blue shoes. They didn't look very nice at all.

"I wish I'd worn my shiny, red shoes," said Angelina and her lip quivered. Angelina's mother gave a big smile and pulled Angelina's shiny, red shoes out of her handbag.

"I brought them along, just in case you changed your mind," her mother said. She sat Angelina down on her knee and helped her take off her scruffy, blue shoes. Then she gave her a huge cuddle and waved goodbye.

Angelina ran inside and had a lovely time at Pippa's party and everybody loved her shiny red shoes.

Where's the Moon?

Robert looked out of the window one night, as his mommy read him a bedtime story. He thought that there was something strange about the sky. Suddenly, Robert realised that there were no stars or moon.

"Where are the stars?" he asked. "Where has the moon gone, Mommy? Are they gone forever, or will they be back soon?" Robert's mom smiled. "Well, maybe they're on their way into the sky," she said. "Why don't we go to the window and have a look?"

Robert stood up and looked out of the window. "The stars are busy putting the sun to bed," his mommy whispered. "But you can call them if you like. All you have to say is, 'Come out stars, come out moon, shine your light, in my bedroom!'"

So, Robert called to the moon and the stars. He asked them to light up his bedroom. As he snuggled down into his bed and fell asleep, he thought he saw a glow outside his window.

Sure enough, the stars and moon had come out at last. Robert slept soundly under starlight and moonbeams all night.

Here We Go Gathering Nuts In May

Here we go gathering nuts in May,
Nuts in May, nuts in May.
Here we go gathering nuts in May,
On a cold and frosty morning.

Who will you have for nuts in May,
Nuts in May, nuts in May?
Who will you have for nuts in May,
On a cold and frosty morning?

Michael Finnegan

There once was a man named Michael Finnegan,
He grew whiskers on his chinigin,
Shaved them off and they grew in again,
Poor old Michael Finnegan.

One Misty Morning

One misty, moisty morning,
When cloudy was the weather.
There I met an old man,
Clothed all in leather.
With cap under his chin,
How do you do, and how do you do,
And how do you do again?

As I Was Going Out

As I was going out one day,
My head fell off and rolled away.
But when I saw that it was gone,
I picked it up and put it on.

And when I got into the street
A fellow cried, "Look at your feet!"
I looked at them and sadly said,
"I've left both asleep in the bed!"

Three Little Monkeys

Three little monkeys jumping on the bed,
One fell off and bumped his head.
Mother called the doctor and the doctor said,
"No more monkeys jumping on the bed!"

Two little monkeys jumping on the bed,
One fell off and bumped his head.
Mother called the doctor and the doctor said,
"No more monkeys jumping on the bed!"

One little monkey jumping on the bed,
He fell off and bumped his head.
Mother called the doctor and the doctor said,
"No more monkeys jumping on the bed!"

Ten Green Bottles

Ten green bottles sitting on the wall,
Ten green bottles sitting on the wall,
And if one green bottle should accidently fall,
There'll be nine green bottles sitting on the wall.

Hokey Pokey

You put your right leg in,
You put your right leg out,
You put your right leg in.
And you shake it all about.
You do the hokey pokey,
And you turn yourself around.
That's what it's all about!

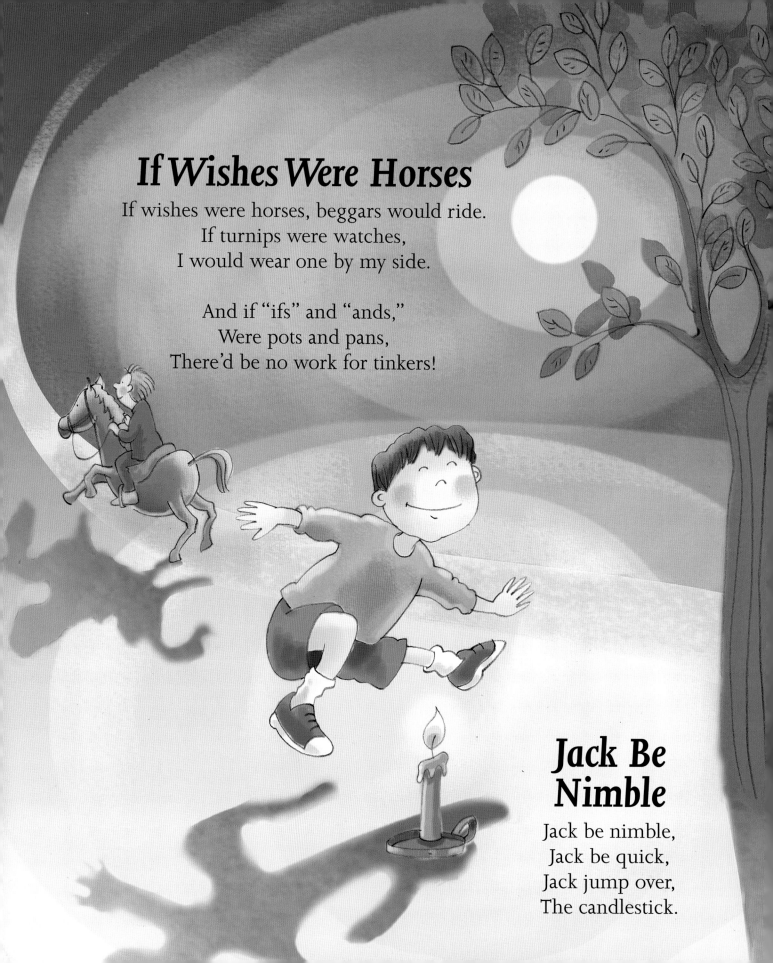

If Wishes Were Horses

If wishes were horses, beggars would ride.
If turnips were watches,
I would wear one by my side.

And if "ifs" and "ands,"
Were pots and pans,
There'd be no work for tinkers!

Jack Be Nimble

Jack be nimble,
Jack be quick,
Jack jump over,
The candlestick.

Engine, Engine

Engine, engine, number nine,
Going down the Chicago line,
If the engine jumps the track,
Will I get my money back?

How Many Miles
To Babylon?

How many miles to Babylon?
Three score and ten.
Can I get there by candlelight?
Aye, and back again.
If your feet are nimble and light,
You'll get there by candlelight.

The Mulberry Bush

Here we go round the mulberry bush,
The mulberry bush, the mulberry bush.
Here we go round the mulberry bush,
So early in the morning.

Mary, Mary

Mary, Mary quite contrary,
How does your garden grow?
With silver bells and cockle shells,
And pretty maids all in a row.

Round And Round The Garden

Round and round the garden,
Like a teddy bear.
One step, two step,
Tickle you under there.

Two Little Dicky Birds

Two little dicky birds,
Sat upon a wall.
One named Peter,
The other named Paul.
Fly away Peter,
Fly away Paul.
Come back Peter,
Come back Paul.

Sing A Song Of Sixpence

Sing a song of sixpence,
A pocket full of rye.
Four-and-twenty blackbirds,
Baked in a pie!

When the pie was opened,
The birds began to sing.
Was not that a dainty dish,
To set before the king?

Cock A Doodle Do

Cock a doodle doo,
My dame has lost her shoe.
My master's lost his fiddling stick
And doesn't know what to do.

Humpty Dumpty

Humpty Dumpty sat on a wall.
Humpty Dumpty had a great fall.
All the King's horses and all the King's men,
Couldn't put Humpty together again.

The Lion And The Unicorn

The lion and the unicorn,
Were fighting for the crown.
The lion beat the unicorn,
All about the town.

Some gave them white bread,
And some gave them brown.
Some gave them plum cake,
And sent them out of town.

Tweedledum And Tweedledee

Tweedledum and Tweedledee,
Agreed to have a battle.
For Tweedledum said Tweedledee,
Had spoilt his nice new rattle.

Just then flew by a monstrous crow,
As big as a tar-barrel.
Which frightened both the heroes so,
Which quite forgot their quarrel.

Three Blind Mice

Three blind mice, three blind mice,
See how they run, see how they run,
They all ran after the farmer's wife,
Who cut their tails with a carving knife,
Did you ever see such a thing in your life,
As three blind mice?

Ladybird

Ladybird, ladybird,
Fly away home.
Your house is on fire,
And your children are all alone.

Thirty Days Hath September

Thirty days hath September,
April, June and November.
All the rest have thirty-one,
Excepting February alone,
For that has twenty-eight days clear,
And twenty-nine in each leap year.

Remember, Remember

Remember, remember,
The fifth of November,
Gunpowder, treason and plot.
I see no reason,
Why gunpowder treason,
Should ever be forgot.

Falling Leaves

All the leaves are falling down,
Orange, yellow, red and brown.
Falling softly as they do,
Over me and over you.
All the leaves are falling down,
Orange, yellow, red and brown.

January Brings The Snow

January brings the snow,
Makes our feet and fingers glow.

February brings the rain,
Thaws the frozen lake again.

March brings breezes sharp and shrill,
Shakes the dancing daffodil.

April brings the primrose sweet,
Scatters daisies at our feet.

May brings flocks of pretty lambs,
Skipping by their fleecy dams.

June brings tulips, lillies, roses,
Fills the children's hands with posies.

Hot July brings cooling showers,
Apricots and gilly flowers.

August brings the sheaves of corn,
Then the harvest home is borne.

Warm September brings the fruit,
Sportsmen then begin to shoot.

Brown October brings the pheasant,
Then to gather nuts is pleasant.

Dull November brings the blast,
Then the leaves go whirling past.

Chill December brings the sleet,
Blazing fire and Christmas treat.

I See The Moon

I see the moon,
And the moon sees me.
I smile at the moon,
And it smiles at me.

Wee Willie Winkie

Wee Willie Winkie,
Runs through the town,
Upstairs and downstairs,
In his nightgown.

Kitty White

Kitty White, so slyly comes,
To catch the mousie gray,
But mousie hears her softly creep,
And quickly runs away!

Boys And Girls Come Out To Play

Girls and boys, come out to play,
The moon doth shine as bright as day.
Leave your supper, and leave your sleep,
And come with your play fellows into the street.
Come with a whoop, come with a call,
Come with a good will, or not at all.
Up the ladder and down the wall,
A halfpenny roll will serve us all.
You find milk, and I'll find flour,
And we'll have a pudding,
In half an hour.

Oranges And Lemons

"Oranges and lemons," say the bells of St. Clement's.
"You owe me five farthings," say the bells of St. Martin's.
"When will you pay me?" say the bells of Old Bailey.
"When I grow rich," say the bells of Shoreditch.
"When will that be?" say the bells of Stepney.
"I do not know," says the great bell at Bow.
"Here comes a candle to light you to bed.
Here comes a chopper to chop off your head.
Chip chop, chip chop, the last man's dead."

Yankee Doodle

Yankee Doodle went to town,
A-riding on a pony.
He stuck a feather in his hat,
And called it macaroni.

Pancake Hat

I went to a party and I brought my hat,
I put it on a bed and along came a cat,
Cat sat down and squashed it flat,
Now I call it my pancake hat.
Pancake hat, pancake hat,
Used to be fine with a feather and that,
Now I call it my pancake hat.

One Potato

One potato, two potato,
Three potato, four.
Five potato, six potato,
Seven potato, more.

Tinker, Tailor

Tinker, tailor,
Soldier, sailor,
Rich man, poor man,
Beggar man,
Thief.

The Cookie Jar

Who stole from the cookie jar?
You stole from the cookie jar.
Who, me? Yes, you!
Couldn't be! Then who?

There Were Ten In The Bed

There were ten in the bed and the little one said,
"Roll over! Roll over!"
So they all rolled over and one fell out.

There were nine in the bed and the little one said,
"Roll over! Roll over!"
So they all rolled over and one fell out.

There were eight in the bed and the little one said,
"Roll over! Roll over!"
So they all rolled over and one fell out.

There were seven in the bed and the little one said,
"Roll over! Roll over!"
So they all rolled over and one fell out.

There were six in the bed and the little one said,
"Roll over! Roll over!"
So they all rolled over and one fell out.

There were five in the bed and the little one said,
"Roll over! Roll over!"
So they all rolled over and one fell out.

There were four in the bed and the little one said,
"Roll over! Roll over!"
So they all rolled over and one fell out.

There were three in the bed and the little one said,
"Roll over! Roll over!"
So they all rolled over and one fell out.

There were two in the bed and the little one said,
"Roll over! Roll over!"
So they all rolled over and one fell out.

There was one in the bed and the little one said,
"Good night!"

Christmas Tree

I'm a little Christmas tree,
Green and bright,
Here is my tinsel, here are my lights,
When I'm all fancy I think I might,
Wait for Santa to come tonight.

Gingerbread

Mix and stir and pat it in the pan,
I'm going to make a gingerbread man.
With a nose so neat,
And a smile so sweet,
And gingerbread shoes,
On his gingerbread feet.

Christmas Is Coming

Christmas is coming, the geese are getting fat,
Please to put a penny in an old man's hat.
If you haven't got a penny a ha'penny will do,
If you haven't got a ha'penny, good wishes to you.

Christmas

Christmas comes,
But once a year.
And when it comes,
It brings good cheer.

Come To The Window

Come to the window,
My baby, with me,
And look at the stars,
That shine on the sea!

Father's Day

"Walk a little slower, Daddy,"
Said a little child so small.
"I'm following in your footsteps
And I don't want to fall!"

Diddle Diddle Dumpling

Diddle diddle dumpling, my son John,
Went to bed with his breeches on.
One stocking off, and one stocking on,
Diddle diddle dumpling, my son John.

The Moon

The moon is round,
As round can be.
Two eyes, a nose and a mouth,
Like me!

Two Little Stars

There are two little stars,
That play bo-peep,
With two little fishes,
Far down in the deep.

And two little frogs,
Cry, "Neap, neap, neap."
I see a dear baby,
That should be asleep.

Twinkle, Twinkle, Little Star

Twinkle, twinkle, little star,
How I wonder what you are.
Up above the world so high,
Like a diamond in the sky.
Twinkle, twinkle, little star,
How I wonder what you are.

Teddy Bears' Picnic

If you go down to the woods today,
You're in for a big surprise.
If you go down to the woods today,
You'll never believe your eyes.
For every bear that ever there was,
Is gathered there for certain because,
Today's the day the teddy bears have their picnic.

Grin And Bear It

When I was just a wee little bear,
My owner dragged me everywhere,
Left me outside in the rain,
Spilled her juice and left this stain.

But I didn't whine or scold,
Because she was only two years old.
And what's a faithful bear to do,
When his little girl is only two?

Fuzzy Wuzzy

Fuzzy Wuzzy was a bear.
Fuzzy Wuzzy had no hair.
So, Fuzzy Wuzzy wasn't really fuzzy,
Was he?

Teddy Bear, Teddy Bear

Teddy bear, teddy bear, turn around,
Teddy bear, teddy bear, touch the ground.
Teddy bear, teddy bear, show your shoe,
Teddy bear, teddy bear, that will do!

Hush Little Baby

Hush little baby, don't say a word,
Mama's gonna buy you a mocking bird.

If that mocking bird don't sing,
Mama's gonna buy you a diamond ring.

If that diamond ring turns brass,
Mama's gonna buy you a looking glass.

Peter Piper

Peter Piper picked a peck of pickled pepper,
A peck of pickled pepper Peter Piper picked.
If Peter Piper picked a peck of picked pepper,
Where's the peck of pickled pepper Peter Piper picked?

Bye, Baby Bunting

Bye, baby bunting,
Daddy's gone a-hunting,
To get a little rabbit skin,
To wrap my baby bunting in.

The Lost Yellow Ball

Ned and Lola had lost their big, yellow ball. It was the best and they really wanted to play with it. They sniffed all over the house to try to find it. Then they sniffed in the garden. Ned spotted something round on the ground in the vegetable patch. "It's our ball!" he said. But when he sniffed it, he realised it was just a smelly, old cabbage.

"I'll look in the shed," said Lola. She opened the door and sniffed around in the gloom. She couldn't see or smell the ball anywhere inside. As she looked harder into the dark, Lola suddenly shrieked. The shed was full of cobwebs and spiders!

Lola bounded out of the shed and across the lawn, to get away from the spiders fast. With one big leap, she jumped over the garden wall. But instead of landing on grass, she stepped on something squashy and soft on the other side.

"It's our big, yellow ball," said Ned. "Well done, Lola, you found it after all." All afternoon, Ned and Lola had fun with their ball. It boinged on the shed and bounced on the wall.

They ran around and giggled, then ran around some more. Ned and Lola were happy. They loved their big, yellow ball.

Alice's Surprise

It was Halloween and Alice and her friends were playing dress up. They having a wonderful time pretending to be wizards and ghosts when suddenly, they saw a spooky shadow outside the door.

"What is it?" asked Pip.
"It sounds like chains clanking," replied Alice.
"What if it's a real ghost?" whispered Max.
At the top of the stairs the strange noise stopped.

Suddenly, there was a loud bump against the bedroom door. Alice screamed. Pip screamed. Max screamed, too! Pip dived under the bed, while Alice jumped into the dressing-up box and Max hid in the wardrobe.

Very slowly, the door began to open. A clinking, clanging shape came stomping into the room.

Alice stared. Pip stared. Max stared, too! Alice thought the shadow looked very familiar. Then, a big, deep voice boomed, "Where is everyone? I've brought you some lemonade and cookies." It was Alice's dad.
"We thought you were a ghost," said Alice.

"No," laughed Dad. "It was just the glasses chinking, as I walked up
the stairs. "Come on, you lot, I think you need a drink and a biscuit after all
that excitement."

So, they all had lemonade and cookies. It had been a very spooky and very
scary Halloween.

The Snoogle Race

It was nearly bedtime on Planet Snoogle, but the little Snoogles weren't tired at all. "Bedtime!" cried Dad, but the naughty Snoogles had other ideas.

"Come on!" they cried. "Let's go for one last whizz around the planets before bedtime!" Then, they all jumped up and down with excitement and dashed off to dive into their spaceships.

With a whizz and a whoosh, they flew up into space. "Whee!" they cried as they circled round Saturn and motored towards Mars. Suddenly, some Martians appeared. They raced the Snoogles all through the sky, shouting, "Ha-ha! Isn't it time you were in bed? Bet we can beat you to Planet Snoogle."

"Oh no you don't," cried the Snoogles. They sped up and zoomed past the Martians. They made a terrible racket, but it was lots of fun.

Suddenly, the Moon shouted, "STOP!" There was a very loud screeching, as the Martians and the Snoogles slammed on their brakes.

"It's far too late to be racing around like this!" said the Moon. "You're making so much noise that you're upsetting the planets and the stars are scared. If the stars are scared they won't twinkle and that just wouldn't be right."

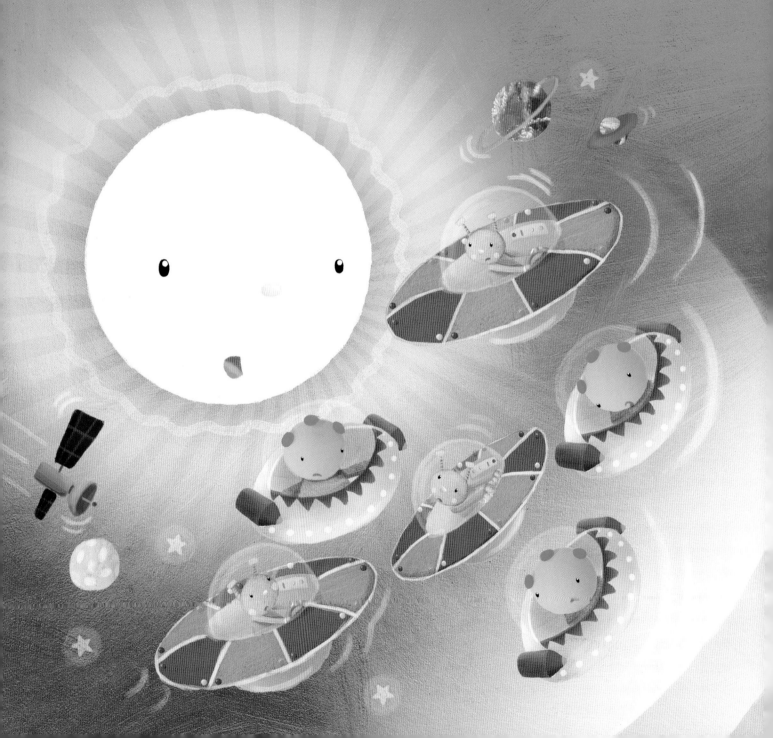

The Martians and the Snoogles all hung their heads. "Sorry, Moon," they said. "Sorry stars and planets. We just wanted to have some fun."

Feeling very sorry and very tired after so much racing, the Martians and Snoogles all went back to their home planets. At last, everyone settled down and the little stars twinkled in the night sky. A hush fell over space, as they all fell asleep. "Goodnight," said the Moon. "Sleep tight."

Helpful Clive

One day, Clive's mother was too busy doing housework to play with Clive. "Maybe if I do things to help her" said Clive, "she'll have time to play with me." So, he went to the cupboard and got the vacuum cleaner. He plugged it in and switched it on.

Suddenly, there was a loud noise and all the flowers in his mother's brown vase disappeared up the long, silvery tube. Then, the vase rocked this way and that and toppled over, onto the carpet. "I don't like the vacuum cleaner," said Clive. He pushed the button again and ran off outside.

Clive thought that he would try watering the vegetable patch. He knew that his mother would find that really helpful.

But as he switched the tap on, the hose flew out of his hand. Water splashed everywhere and Clive got completely soaked. He slipped and slid around on the wet grass, finally falling over into the muddy vegetable patch.

Clive's best friend, Ned, had been standing at the gate and seen all of this happen. He giggled. "Oh, Clive," he said. "You're very muddy. You'd better go and tell your mother."

Just then Clive heard his mother's voice calling. "What have you been doing, Clive? My flowers have gone, the vase is broken and the carpet's all wet!"

Clive slunk into the kitchen, dripping. "I just wanted to help, so you'd have time to play with me," he said and he began to cry.

"Thank you, Clive," soothed his mother, in her softest voice. "You're a bit small to do housework all by yourself. Perhaps, next time, we'll do it together."

That afternoon, after Clive had put on some nice, dry clothes, mother made some extra-special, delicious cookies. Ned came round and they all had lots of fun. Being helpful was all very well, but it wasn't nearly as exciting as playing hide-and-seek.

The Farm Girl and Her Dog

Once upon a time, there was an orphan girl who lived and worked on a farm, with the help of her faithful old sheepdog. One day, however, the farmer told the girl that he had sold the farm. So the girl had to leave, with no money and nowhere to go.

The girl cried as she left the farm, scared of what would happen to her now. Her faithful old sheepdog left with her. As they stepped onto the country road, something miraculous happened. "Don't cry, mistress," said the dog. "I can help you."

The farm girl was amazed that the dog could talk. She had worked with him all those years and he had never said a word. "Far away from here," said the dog, "there is a grand palace, with warm beds and all the food you can eat. If you will come with me, I will show you the way."

The farm girl thought for a while. She had no one else that she could trust to take care of her, so she agreed and followed the sheepdog. Soon, they could see the palace, on a steep hill in the distance.

They reached the palace grounds, but between them and the palace itself stood a vast maze. Together, the dog and the farm girl entered the maze. They wandered for a long time before they finally reached the center. There, a huge, brown lion stood guard. It gave a menacing roar when it saw them.

Suddenly, the sheepdog began to grow. He turned into a golden lion. The two lions fought with all their might, until the golden lion was knocked to the floor.

The farm girl knew she had to save her friend, so she ran up to the brown lion and pulled his tail as hard as she could. The brown lion yelped as the golden lion jumped from under its grasp. Then, the golden lion roared so fiercely that the brown lion ran away.

When the farm girl turned around to see the golden lion, she gasped in surprise. He had turned into a handsome prince. The prince took her hand. "This is my palace," he said. "I was cursed by my own selfishness and greed to be a humble dog, until I could truly help someone without asking for anything in return."

The farm girl took one look at the prince and fell in love. The prince loved her too and they were soon married. They lived in safety and happiness in the palace for the rest of their lives.

Don't Worry Wanda

Wanda worried about everything, all the time. She worried about her
schoolwork and about her pets and about what her mom would cook for tea
every night. She couldn't help finding new things to worry about wherever
she went. Wanda wanted to have fun at the park so badly, but all she could do
was worry!

Wanda was on the roundabout at the park. Round and round it whizzed and swished. But Wanda was worried that it would go too fast.

"I feel dizzy," she wailed, "I want to get off."
"Don't worry, Wanda," said Mom. "We'll try the swings instead."

The park swing went back and forth. But Wanda was worried that it would go too high. Her little chin quivered and she began to cry.

"My tummy feels funny and I want to get off," she sobbed. "Don't worry, Wanda," said Mom and she took her hand. "We'll try the slide instead."

At the slide, Mom said, "I'll hold your hand. Let's count to three." So, Mom counted one, two, three and Wanda slid all the way to the bottom.

"That was fun!" cried Wanda. "Can I do it again?"

Very soon, Wanda was sliding down all by herself and Mom was very pleased. "You see, Wanda," she said, "there's really no need to worry at all."

Wanda spent the rest of the day playing at the park. She made lots of new friends and, best of all, she stopped worrying so much! .

Nigel's Brush

It was painting day at Nigel's house. Nigel loved to paint better than anything else. He even had special overalls to wear when he painted his pictures.

Mom put a new sheet of paper on the easel. Nigel got out his big, special brush. He was just about to dip into some paint when the telephone rang. "Wait a minute, Nigel," said Mom as she went into the hall.

But Nigel didn't want to wait. With a gloop and a splosh he dipped his big, special brush into a pot of pink paint and went SPLODGE, onto the clean, white paper.

"This is great fun!" said Nigel, swishing his brush. Then, he cleaned it in a glass of water and dipped it into another pot of paint. Nigel giggled and splashed and splatted all the bright paints in his big, paint tray onto the paper..

Then, Mom came back in. Her eyes grew wide. "Nigel!" she cried. "I told you to wait. You're covered in paint!"

"I drew a picture of you, Mommy," said Nigel, with a smile.
Mom sighed and then she smiled, too. "Thank you, Nigel," she said. "That's very kind of you. But I think we need to go upstairs and get you cleaned up."

Mom took Nigel upstairs. "Take off those dirty dungarees," she said, "and jump into this nice, soapy bath."

"If it rains, can we do painting tomorrow, Mommy?" asked Nigel. "Yes, Nigel," said Mom, "but next time, we'll do it together!"

Franky's Shadow

Franky had a lovely blue bedroom that he slept in all by himself. He loved bedtime, but one night, Franky had a very bad dream. So, he got out of bed and crept along the landing to his mom and dad's room. But, something very scary was following Franky. He spotted it out of the corner of his eye and gasped.

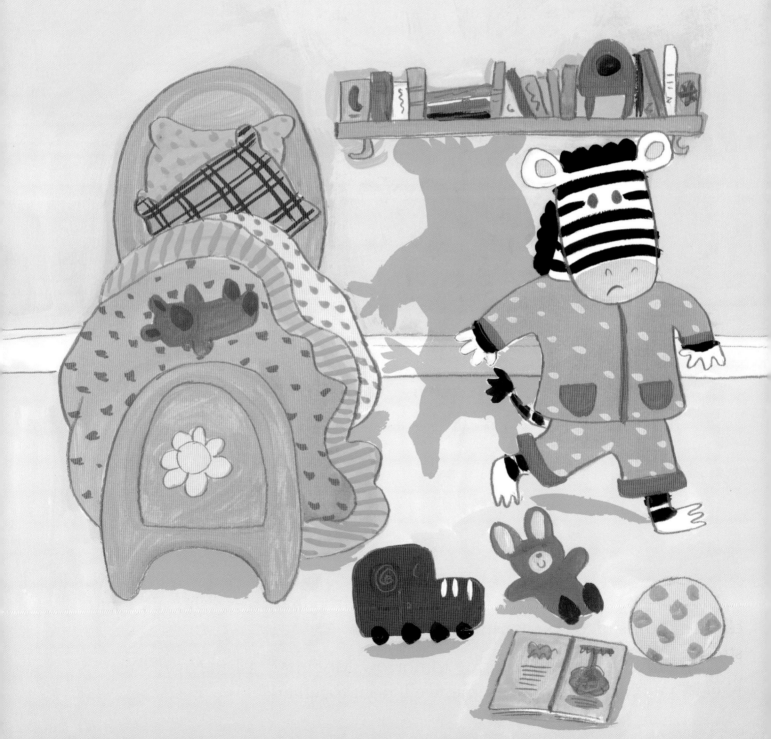

It was big and grey and had arms and legs. It looked like it had very long claws, too. When Franky moved, it moved, too. When Franky stood still, it stood still, too. It followed him all the way down the corridor as he walked. Franky didn't like the strange shape that was following him.

"Mommy!" cried Franky, at the top of his voice. "There's a monster following me. Help!"

Mom and Dad came running out of their bedroom, looking very worried. Mom looked at the big, grey shape. "It's not a monster," she said, laughing. "It's just your shadow and it's nothing to be afraid of."

"Oh, a shadow!" said Franky. "I still had a scary dream, though. Can I come and stay with you tonight?"

"Alright, just for tonight," said Mom and Dad. They let Franky snuggle up with them in their bed. Franky felt a lot braver now he knew that there wasn't a monster chasing him. And after that night, he never had bad dreams again.

The Weather Witch

Peter and Polly lived in a little village surrounded by bright golden cornfields. Each year, the people of the village harvested the corn and milled it in the old windmill by the brook.

One summer, no rain came and the crops stopped growing. Peter and Polly asked their father what would happen. "If it does not rain, the seeds will not grow," their father said. "There will be no harvest and we shall starve. Some might say it is time to call on the Weather Witch."

Peter and Polly wanted to know all about the Weather Witch, so their father told them. "The tale of The Weather Witch is one that is told to children when the harvest fails, so listen carefully.

"No one has ever seen The Weather Witch, but it is said that she controls the wind and the rain. She sends storms when she is angry and soft rain when she is at peace. I have heard folk say that she lives in a cave, under a waterfall many days journey from here."

The very next day, Peter and Polly set out to find the Weather Witch. They were walking through a field when they saw a cat with a field mouse in its paws. "Help me!" cried the mouse, "or I'll be eaten!"

Peter scared the cat away and the mouse thanked them. "I have no gold, or silver," said the mouse, "but maybe I can help you, too, one day?"

That night, the two children slept on the cold forest ground.
Something tickled Peter's nose and woke him up. It was a big, shiny
green beetle and Peter went to brush the beetle off, but it said,
"Please, don't turn me away. It's very cold out here. Can I sleep next
to you tonight?"

Peter didn't like the idea of sleeping next to a beetle, but he was
too kindhearted to refuse and he let the little creature settle next
to him. In the morning, the beetle thanked Peter and said, "I have no
gold, or silver, but maybe I can help you, too, one day?"

Peter and Polly continued on their way and reached a waterfall. Behind the waterfall was a dark cave. In the shadows, hunched over, sat the Weather Witch. "What do you want?" she said, grumpily.

The children told the witch that they needed rain for their harvest. The Weather Witch laughed and it sounded like a crack of thunder. "I will send rain to your village if you bring me two impossible things. A singing stone and a living jewel," she said, slinking back into the darkness of her cave.

Peter and Polly thought about the Weather Witch's words. "What she asks is impossible," said Peter. "It's hopeless," signed Polly. Suddenly, Peter felt something tugging at his sleeve. It was the mouse that they had rescued from the cat.

"I can help you," said the mouse. It scampered off, then returned with something in its paws. It was a stone with a hole in the middle. The children took the stone to the Weather Witch. When they held it up, the cold wind blew through it and made a low whistling sound.

"A stone that sings," said the witch. "You have done well, but what about my living jewel?" She sent the children back outside, where they sat wondering how they could possibly find a living jewel.

The children sat outside the cave thinking. This time, the big green beetle crawled up to them. "I would love to help you," it said, "but I have no secrets and no skill."

"Wait," said Polly. "You are the brightest green I have ever seen. You look just like a living jewel." They took the beetle into the cave, where the wind was roaring even more strongly than before. They showed the bright, shiny green beetle to the Weather Witch.

The Weather Witch took the beetle. She started to shake and make a deep, booming sound. The children got ready to run away, but then they realised that she was laughing. "You children are very clever!" chortled the Weather Witch. She handed them a glass ball. "Return to your village and break
this ball."

When Peter and Polly reached their village after many days' travel, nobody believed them when they told their tale. Then the children threw the glass ball onto the ground, breaking it. Great, grey clouds spilled from the broken ball, filling the sky and a gentle rain began to fall.

"It's true!" said their father, hugging them both. That year, the crops grew higher than ever. The villagers had more than enough bread to eat and Peter and Polly lived happily ever after.

Goodnight, Bradley

Bradley was looking at his new space monster book. He asked his mother earlier if there were really monsters who lived in outer space. Bradley was scared that they might be able to get into his room at night.

"No, there's no such thing," his mother had replied. "Come on now, it's bedtime. You go upstairs and I'll come and tuck you in."

That night, the wind blew clouds across the moon and rattled Bradley's window. He looked outside at the shadows and shapes. "What if space monsters really do exist?" whispered Bradley. "What if they come from the moon, into my room?"

Just then, Bradley heard a shuffle on the stairs and saw a shadow stretch up over the banister and along the wall. "Is that you, Mom?" whispered Bradley, in a small, scared voice. But no one answered. So, Bradley sunk right down into his bed and pulled his quilt up to his chin. "Are you a space monster?" he called out, bravely.

"No, Bradley," said his mother's soft, laughing voice. "It's me, and I've come to tuck you in, kiss you goodnight and tell you a story. But not one about space monsters!"

Bradley was very relieved. He still loved space monsters, but he was glad that they only existed in books.

Charlie and the Cookies

Charlie loved cookies. He thought the best ones were the crunchy and buttery ones with delicious dollops of chocolate inside. Each night after tea, Mom let Charlie have a cookie as a treat. Charlie always wanted another one, but Mom said, "No, Charlie, you shouldn't eat too many cookies."

One night, Charlie saw that Mom had forgotten to put the cookie jar back in the cupboard. "I'll just have a little taste," he said, reaching inside. He chewed and munched and soon a whole cookie was gone. So, Charlie took another and then another. Then, with his tummy all full, he crept upstairs to bed.

Later, Mom went into the kitchen and found cookie crumbs all over the floor. She followed a trail of crumbs that led all the way upstairs.

In Charlie's room, there were some very strange sounds coming from under the quilt. "Ooh, ow, ouch," groaned a little voice. "What's the matter, Charlie?" asked Mom. "I've got stomach ache," replied Charlie, coming out from under the covers.

Mom smiled and said very softly, "Well, Charlie, now you know why it's not good to eat too many cookies."

Luckily, Mom had some special medicine to make Charlie's tummy-ache go away. Soon, he was settled down in bed, all comfy and warm. "Thank you, Mommy," said Charlie, as he drifted off to sleep.

Mom gently kissed him goodnight and she turned out the light. After that, Charlie never ate too many cookies again.

Night Night, Fred

It was time for bed at Fred's house. "Come on, Fred,"
said Dad. "The sun's asleep and the moon is bright.
It's time to put away your toys and say goodnight."

But Fred didn't want to go to bed. He wanted to play with his toys. "No," he said.
"Come on, now," said Dad and he held out his arms.

But Fred took two steps back and he shook his head and his cheeks went red. "No bed," he said.

"Well," sighed Dad. "Let's play a game instead. Let's pretend the toys are tired after the day. But they can't go to sleep until they're put away. Could you help me to tuck them up in the toy box and say goodnight?"

Fred looked at his toys and he looked at Dad. Then he thought for a while and said, "Alright."

Fred picked up his toys and he kissed them goodnight . Dad closed the lid of the toy box tight. Fred gave a sigh and he rubbed his eyes. "I'm tired," he said.
"Come on," whispered Dad and he gently picked up Fred and laid him in his bed.

After all those goodnight kisses, Fred was suddenly very sleepy after all. Outside, the moon shone bright, but Fred didn't see it. As soon as he snuggled up under his quilt, he had fallen fast asleep!

The Golden Boots

A long time ago, there lived a boy prince who loved to dance. Each day, he practiced his steps with a little serving girl called Carrie. The boy prince and the serving girl became the best of friends and danced all over the palace.

One day, however, the king told his son that he could not dance with Carrie any more. "She is just a serving girl," he said. "And you are a prince. You must play with princesses."

Years passed and the prince and the serving girl grew up. The prince gave splendid balls and parties at the palace and everyone danced all night. However, the king would not allow the prince to invite Carrie. She had to work in the kitchens and serve the food at the splendid banquets.

Soon, the time came for the prince to marry. "I shall marry the girl who is the best dancer," he said. "I do not care how rich, or poor she is. Tomorrow, a banquet will be held in my honor. Afterwards, there will be a dancing competition. Whoever wins it will become my bride."

The prince secretly hoped that Carrie would enter the competition. He had not forgotten how beautifully she had danced when they were children. If she won it, his father, the king, could do nothing to stop them marrying.

Soon, the palace was full of girls practicing their dancing. Carrie watched from the shadows, as they whirled and twirled in their ball gowns. "I cannot possibly hope to dance like they do," she said, sadly. "They are so elegant and beautiful."

Carrie had to clear up after the banquet. As she was walking back to the kitchen, an old lady came up to her. "I am a poor, old woman, with no food," said the old lady. "Can you spare me some bread?"

The serving girl handed the woman some food and she ate it, hungrily. "In return," said the old woman, "I will give you my golden boots. The person who wears them will dance better than anyone else because they are enchanted. You deserve them for being kind."

Carrie thanked the old lady and put on the golden boots. That night, she danced with the prince, far better than any of the other girls in the palace. "This girl will be my bride!" cried the prince joyfully, and they were married the very next day.

Carrie was so happy. She never forgot about the old lady who had given her the boots. She even wore the boots under her wedding dress. She danced and danced at the wedding celebrations and her and her prince lived happily ever after.

Tomboy Tina

Tina's mom was having a party. "Cousin Zara is coming early to play," she said. "Do you want to put on a dress and some shoes?"

But, Tina just shook her head. "I don't want a dress, or shoes," she said. "I want to wear my scruffy dungarees, so I can climb up trees."

Cousin Zara arrived a few minutes later. Her outfit sparkled like stars, covered in glitter and spangles. She wore a fancy hairband and red, jingly bracelets. Zara twirled around on her tiptoes and it seemed to Tina that she was just like a fairy, or a ballerina.

The cousins went to play in Tina's bedroom. Tina showed Zara her favorite green dungarees, while she looked at Zara's pretty pink flip-flops.

"I love your dungarees," said Zara. "They're so nice and bright!" Tina giggled. She thought Zara looked lovely, too. The cousins played together in the garden.

They danced and skipped, Tina in her dungarees and Zara in her princess dress. "We make the perfect duo," said Zara, laughing.

Tina's mom brought out yummy cupcakes and sandwiches. It was the most fun afternoon Tina had ever had, and for once she was proud of her muddy dungarees.

Bedtime For Ted

It was night-time in Edward's house, but he didn't want to go to bed. He couldn't find Little Ted, his favorite teddy bear. Edward knew that he couldn't sleep without him. "I'm not going to sleep," he said to his dad, "Not without Little Ted." Dad and Edward looked high and low, searching Edward's room for Little Ted, but they simply couldn't find him anywhere.

They looked in all of the cupboards and drawers, but still didn't know where Little Ted had gone. Then, Edward's dad pointed at the bed and said, "Look!"

He had spotted a little furry head under Edward's quilt. "I've found your teddy, Edward," said Edward's dad, laughing. "He's been in your bed ready to go to sleep all along!"

"Naughty Little Ted," said Edward. "You were hiding from us for ages, weren't you?" Edward tried to be angry at Little Ted, but he couldn't stay cross for long. He gave Little Ted a big cuddle. "Thank you for finding him," said Edward to his dad, with a smile.

Edward snuggled down under his quilt with Little Ted wrapped safely in his arms. "Goodnight, Little Ted. Goodnight, Edward," said Dad, as he tucked them both into bed.

But there was no reply. Edward and Little Ted had already fallen fast asleep.

Banbury Cross

Ride a cock-horse,
To Banbury Cross,
To see an old lady,
Upon a white horse.

Rings on her fingers,
And bells on her toes.
She shall have music,
Wherever she goes.

Race Horse

One-one was a race horse.
Two-two was one too.
One-one won one race.
Two-two won one too.

Slow Bunny

Did you ever see a bunny, a bunny, a bunny,
Did you ever see a bunny that hops so slow?
He hops, and hops, and hops, and hops,
Did you ever see a bunny that hops so slow?

Little Betty Blue

Little Betty Blue lost her holiday shoe.
What can little Betty do?
Give her another to match the other,
And then she may walk in two.

Pins

See a pin and pick it up,
All the day you'll have good luck.
See a pin and let it lay,
Bad luck you'll have all the day.

Little Boys

What are little boys made of?
What are little boys made of?
Slugs and snails,
And puppy dog tails,
That's what little boys are made of.

Monday's Child

Monday's child is fair of face,
Tuesday's child is full of grace,
Wednesday's child is full of woe,
Thursday's child has far to go,
Friday's child is loving and giving,
Saturday's child must work hard for a living,
But the child who is born on the Sabbath day,
Is bonny and blithe and good and gay.

Little Girls

What are little girls made of?
What are little girls made of?
Sugar and spice,
And all things nice.
That's what little girls are made of.

All Work
And No Play

All work and no play,
Makes Jack a dull boy.
All play and no work,
Makes Jack a mere toy.

Here We Go Looby Loo

Here we go looby loo,
Here we go looby light,
Here we go looby loo,
All on a Saturday night.

Daffy Down Dilly

Daffy down dilly,
Has come to town.
In a yellow petticoat,
And a green gown.

The Bunch Of Blue Ribbons

Oh, dear, what can the matter be?
Oh, dear, what can the matter be?
Oh, dear, what can the matter be?
Johnny's so long at the fair.

He promised he'd buy me a bunch of blue ribbons,
He promised he'd buy me a bunch of blue ribbons,
He promised he'd buy me a bunch of blue ribbons,
To tie up my bonnie brown hair.

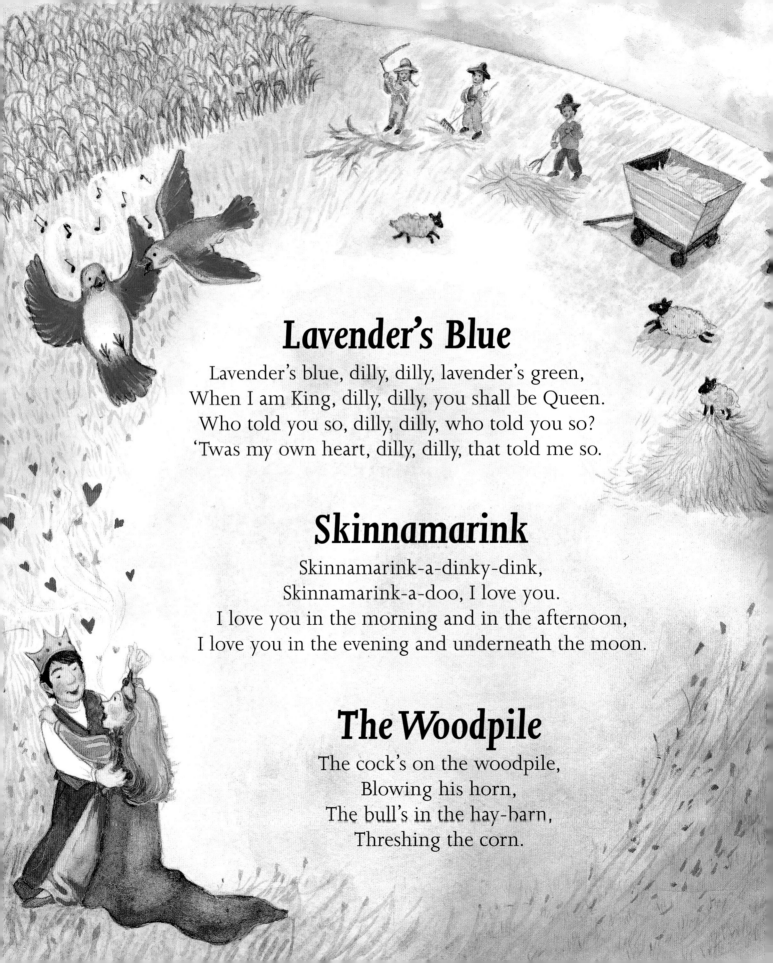

Lavender's Blue

Lavender's blue, dilly, dilly, lavender's green,
When I am King, dilly, dilly, you shall be Queen.
Who told you so, dilly, dilly, who told you so?
'Twas my own heart, dilly, dilly, that told me so.

Skinnamarink

Skinnamarink-a-dinky-dink,
Skinnamarink-a-doo, I love you.
I love you in the morning and in the afternoon,
I love you in the evening and underneath the moon.

The Woodpile

The cock's on the woodpile,
Blowing his horn,
The bull's in the hay-barn,
Threshing the corn.

Little Cock Sparrow

A little cock sparrow sat on a green tree,
And he chirruped, he chirruped, so merry was he.
A naughty boy came with his wee bow and arrow,
Determined to shoot this little cock sparrow.

"This little cock sparrow shall make me a stew,
And his giblets shall make me a little pie too."
"Oh, no," said the sparrow, "I won't make a stew!"
So he flapped his wings, and away he flew.

I Saw Three Ships

I saw three ships come sailing by,
Come sailing by, come sailing by,
I saw three ships come sailing by,
On New Year's Day in the morning.

And what do you think was in them then,
Was in them then, was in them then?
And what do you think was in them then,
On New Year's Day in the morning?

The Animals Went In

The animals went in two by two,
Hurrah, hurrah!
The animals went in two by two,
Hurrah, hurrah!
The animals went in two by two,
The elephant and the kangaroo,
And they all went into the ark,
For to get out of the rain.

Bobby Shaftoe

Bobby Shaftoe went to sea,
Silver buckles on his knee.
He'll come back and marry me,
Pretty Bobby Shaftoe.

Bobby Shaftoe's fine and fair,
Combing down his auburn hair.
He's my friend for ever more,
Pretty Bobby Shaftoe.

Rub-A-Dub

Rub-a-dub-dub,
Three men in a tub,
And who do you think they be?
The butcher, the baker,
The candlestick maker.
They all sailed out to sea.

Bow-Wow

"Bow-wow," says the dog,
"Mew, mew," says the cat,
"Grunt, grunt," goes the hog,
And, "Squeak," goes the rat.

Chirp, Chirp

"Chirp, chirp," says the sparrow,
"Caw, caw," says the crow,
"Quack, quack," says the duck,
And what cuckoos say, you know.

Windscreen Wipers

The windscreen wipers on our car,
Are busy when it rains.
They swing and swing,
Clup-clup, clup-clup,
Then back and forth again.

If All The World

If all the world were apple pie,
And all the sea were ink.
And all the trees were bread and cheese,
What would we have to drink?

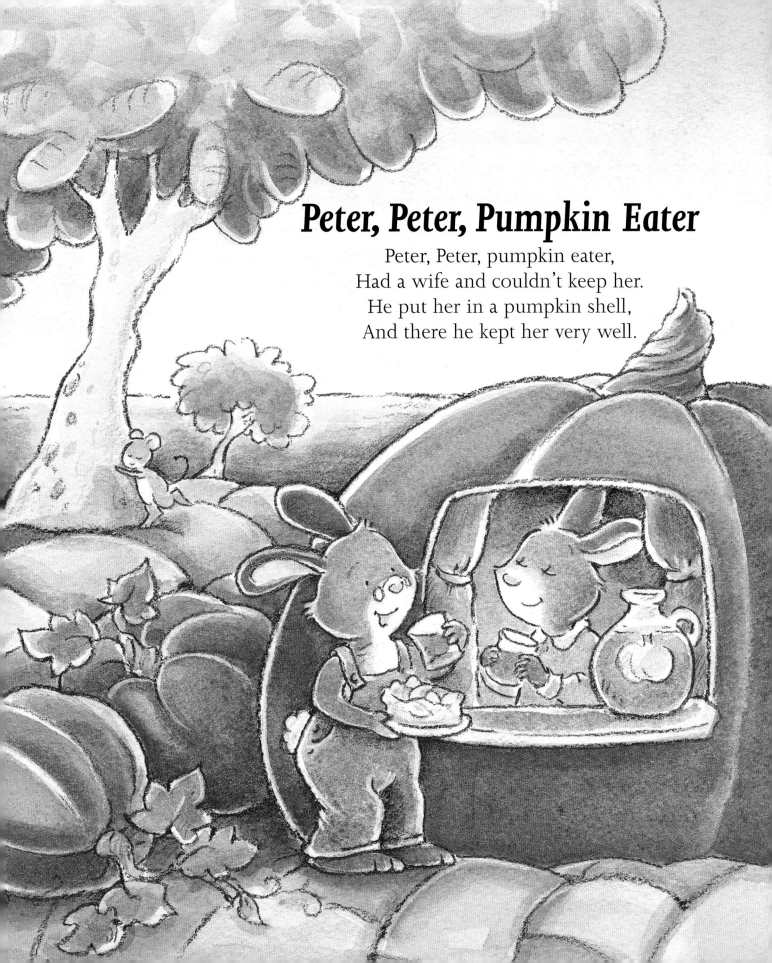

Peter, Peter, Pumpkin Eater

Peter, Peter, pumpkin eater,
Had a wife and couldn't keep her.
He put her in a pumpkin shell,
And there he kept her very well.

Daisy Daisy

Daisy, Daisy, give me your answer do.
I'm half crazy all for the love of you.
It won't be a stylish marriage,
I can't afford a carriage.
But you'll look sweet,
Upon the seat,
Of a bicycle made for two.

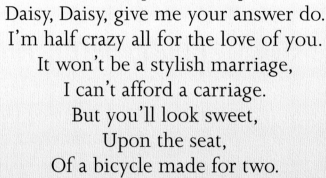

A Cat And A Mouse

A cat and a mouse and a bumble-bee,
Started a-dancing, one, two, three.
They danced in the daytime,
They danced in the night,
They cared not whether it was dark or light.

Vintery, Mintery

Vintery, mintery, cutery, corn,
Apple seed and apple thorn,
Wire, briar, limber lock,
Three geese in a flock.

One flew east,
And one flew west,
And one flew over,
The cuckoo's nest.

Tommy Tittlemouse

Little Tommy Tittlemouse,
Lived in a little house.
He caught fishes,
In other men's ditches.

One, Two, Buckle My Shoe

One, two,
Buckle my shoe.

Three, four,
Knock at the door.

Five, six,
Pick up sticks.

Seven, eight,
Lay them straight.

Nine, ten,
A good, fat hen.

Eleven, twelve,
Dig and delve.

Thirteen, fourteen,
Maids a-courting.

Fifteen, sixteen,
Maids in the kitchen.

Seventeen, eighteen,
Maids a-waiting.

Nineteen, twenty,
My plate's empty.

Here Is The Church

Here is the church,
Here is the steeple,
Open the doors,
And see all the people.

Elsie Marley

Elsie Marley is grown so fine,
She won't get up,
To feed the swine.
But lies in bed,
Till eight or nine,
Lazy Elsie Marley.

Frère Jacques

Frère Jacques.
Frère Jacques.

Dormez vous?
Dormez vous?

Sonnez les matines.
Sonnez les matines.

Ding, dang, dong.
Ding, dang, dong.

Fee, Fie, Foe, Fum!

Fee, Fie, Foe, Fum!
I smell the blood of an Englishman.
Be he alive, or be he dead,
I'll grind his bones to make my bread.

Eenie, Meenie, Minie, Mo

Eenie, meenie, minie, mo,
Catch a tiger by the toe.
If he hollers let him go,
Eenie, meenie, minie, mo.

Sippity, Sippity Sup

Sippity sup, sippity sup,
Bread and milk from a china cup.
Bread and milk from a bright silver spoon,
Made of a piece of the bright silver moon.
Sippity sup, sippity sup,
Sippity, sippity sup.

Mix A Pancake

Mix a pancake,
Stir a pankcake,
Pop it in the pan.
Fry the pancake,
Toss the pankcake,
Catch it if you can.

Bow, Wow, Wow

Bow, wow, wow,
Whose dog art thou?
Little Tom Tinker's dog,
Bow, wow, wow.

My Grandfather's Clock

My Grandfather's clock,
Was too large for the shelf,
So it stood ninety years on the floor.
It was taller by half,
Than the old man himself,
Though it weighed
not a pennyweight more.
It was bought on the morn,
Of the day he was born,
And was always his treasure
and pride,
But it stopped short,
Never to go again,
When the old man died.

Hickory Dickory Dock

Hickory dickory dock,
The mouse ran up the clock.
The clock struck one,
The mouse ran down,
Hickory dickory dock.

Once I Saw A Little Bird

Once I saw a little bird,
Go hop, hop, hop.
So I cried, little bird,
Will you stop, stop, stop?
And I was going to the window,
To say, how do you do?
When he shook his little tail,
And away he flew.

Horsie, Horsie

Horsie, horsie, don't you stop,
Just let your feet go clippety clop.
Your tail goes swish,
And the wheels go round,
Giddyup, you're homeward bound!

For Want Of A Nail

For want of a nail the shoe was lost.
For want of a shoe the horse was lost.
For want of a horse the rider was lost.
For want of a rider the battle was lost.
For want of a battle the kingdom was lost.
And all for the want of a horseshoe nail.

Cobbler, Cobbler

Cobbler, cobbler, mend my shoe.
Get it done by half-past two.
Stitch it up and stitch it down,
And then I'll give you half a crown.

If You're Happy And You Know It

If you're happy and you know it,
Clap your hands.
If you're happy and you know it,
Clap your hands.
If you're happy and you know it,
And you really want to show it,
If you're happy and you know it,
Clap your hands.

Old Mother Twitchett

Old Mother Twitchett had but one eye,
And a long tail which she let fly,
And every time she went through a gap,
A bit of her tail she left in a trap.

There Was An Old Woman

There was an old woman,
Who lived in a shoe.
She had so many children,
She didn't know what to do.
She gave them some broth,
Without any bread.
She whipped them all soundly,
And sent them to bed.

The Cats Went Out

The cats went out to serenade,
And on a banjo sweetly played,
And summer nights they climbed a tree,
And sang, "My love, oh, come to me!"

Little Robin Redbreast

Little Robin Redbreast sat upon a tree,
Up went pussy cat, and down went he!
Down came pussy, and away Robin ran,
Says little Robin Redbreast, "Catch me if you can!"

This Old Man

This old man, he played one,
He played knick knack on my thumb.
With a knick knack paddy whack,
Give a dog a bone.
This old man came rolling home.

Head, Shoulders, Knees And Toes

Head, shoulders,
Knees and toes, knees and toes,
Head, shoulders,
Knees and toes, knees and toes,
And eyes and ears,
And mouth and nose,
Head, shoulders, knees and toes,
Knees and toes.

Do Your Ears Hang Low?

Do your ears hang low?
Do they wobble to and fro?
Can you tie 'em in a knot?
Can you tie 'em in a bow?

Do your ears flip flop?
Can you use them as a mop?
Are they stringy at the bottom?
Are they curly at the top?

Does your tongue hang out?
Can you shake it all about?
When you try to tuck it in,
Does it just hang out?

I Wriggle My Fingers

I wriggle my fingers,
I wriggle my toes.
I wriggle my shoulders,
I wriggle my nose.
No more wriggles,
Are left in me,
So I will be as still as can be.

Jack A Nory

I'll tell you a story about Jack A Nory,
And now my story's told.
I'll tell you another,
About Jack and his brother,
And now my story's done.